WORD TO THE WISE

Center Point
Large Print

Also by Jenn McKinlay and available from
Center Point Large Print:

About a Dog
Barking Up the Wrong Tree
Death in the Stacks
Every Dog Has His Day
Hitting the Books

**This Large Print Book carries the
Seal of Approval of N.A.V.H.**

WORD
TO THE
WISE

Jenn McKinlay

CENTER POINT LARGE PRINT
THORNDIKE, MAINE

This Center Point Large Print edition
is published in the year 2019 by arrangement with
Berkley, an imprint of Penguin Publishing Group,
a division of Penguin Random House LLC.

This is a work of fiction. Names, characters, places,
and incidents either are the product of the author's
imagination or are used fictitiously, and any resemblance
to actual persons, living or dead, business establishments,
events, or locales is entirely coincidental.

PUBLISHER'S NOTE: The recipes contained in this
book are to be followed exactly as written. The publisher
is not responsible for your specific health or allergy needs
that may require medical supervision. The publisher is
not responsible for any adverse reactions to the recipes
contained in this book.

The text of this Large Print edition is unabridged.
In other aspects, this book may vary
from the original edition.
Printed in the United States of America
on permanent paper.
Set in 16-point Times New Roman type.

ISBN: 978-1-64358-369-3

The Library of Congress has cataloged this record under
Library of Congress Control Number: 2019946298

In loving memory of Jen Dunbar Heth,
a person my husband so aptly describes
as the best of us. Through you,
I learned what it means to have courage,
to find big joy in small things,
and to live every day with love.
You were the embodiment of grace
and yet greeted life's challenges with
a warrior's fortitude. Although you didn't
want to go, you couldn't stay, but you will
remain forever in our hearts.

Acknowledgments

Big thanks to Kate Seaver, Sarah Blumenstock and Christina Hogrebe for their endless support and encouragement, as well as their invaluable input. You help make my books the best they can be and I am ever grateful. Also, I am so pleased to have such a tremendous team at Berkley—Tara O'Connor and Jessica Mangicaro. And, as always, I am thrilled to have cover artist Julia Green use her tremendous talent to make my book covers real showstoppers.

Special thanks to Detective Armstrong of the Phoenix Police Department. You were invaluable in helping me when no one else would listen. The city of Phoenix is lucky to have you.

And, as always, big thanks to my family and friends, who put up with burnt dinner, no dinner, piles of laundry, canceled plans and the occasional author meltdown with kindness, understanding and humor. I love you all—most especially Chris Hansen Orf, Wyatt Orf and Beckett Orf, who have to live with me. Poor bastards.

1

"Too meringue, too low-cut, holy bananas, too high-cut!" Lindsey Norris sat at the reference desk of the Briar Creek Public Library and clicked through a website full of wedding dresses. Her mother had sent her the link in an email and wanted to know what sort of dress Lindsey was thinking of wearing for her upcoming wedding. Too many choices. There were just too many. She felt herself starting to melt down, so she closed the website. She'd get back to her mother on this soon. Really, she would.

It was the height of summer in Briar Creek, and she had a good five months before the wedding. It was going to be a very small holiday ceremony out on Bell Island, one of the Thumb Islands that made up the archipelago of over one hundred islands—some were just big rocks—in the bay off Briar Creek's shore. Her fiancé, Captain Mike Sullivan, had asked that they get married on the island where he'd grown up, and Lindsey couldn't think of a more romantic place to say "I do." So the location was a go. It was all the other details that were killing her.

Click click click.

Lindsey turned around to see a bat fluttering through the book stacks. She was a pretty big bat. With large ears pointing up from a wide headband and enormous pale gray wings made out of an old bedsheet and some wire, she fluttered her outspread arms while holding a mango in one hand. She also had merry eyes and shoulder-length dark brown hair and answered to the name of Beth Barker. She was the Briar Creek children's librarian, and she was leading a parade of toddlers and their parents through the library, all fluttering their "wings" and making clicking noises.

Lindsey propped her chin on her hand as she watched the little bats flutter by. She met Beth's happy gaze and said, "Practicing your echolocation, Stellaluna?"

Beth grinned and said, "Naturally, then it's back to the bat cave to read *Nightsong* and *Bat Loves the Night*."

"Flutter on," Lindsey said.

"Will do. Don't forget crafternoon is today," Beth said. "We're making tin can lanterns. And for the food, I ran with the Chicana theme since we are discussing *The House on Mango Street*."

"Can't wait. I love that book," Lindsey said. Which was true, plus she had also seen the food that Beth had brought for lunch, and there were quesadillas, mango smoothies and flan. There was just nothing better than flan on a hot summer day.

"Okay, little bats," Beth said. "Let's get back to the cave. *Click click.*"

Lindsey watched as Beth led her colony of bats and their parents back to the story time room. Then she glanced at the circulation desk to see Ms. Cole watching the commotion over the top of her reading glasses. Nicknamed "the lemon" for her occasional puckered disposition, Ms. Cole had come a long way since Lindsey had been hired as the library director several years ago. Instead of chastising Beth, she simply heaved a put-upon sigh, which was encouraging.

The lemon had lightened up on late fees, beverages in the building and the exuberance of the story time regulars, but the one policy on which Ms. Cole did not bend was noise. She was a shusher of the first order, and Lindsey was surprised she hadn't hissed at Beth to keep it down. Instead, Ms. Cole put her left index finger over her left eyelid as if trying to prevent it from twitching. Lindsey glanced down at the top of her desk to keep from laughing.

"Excuse me."

Lindsey turned her head to see a man standing at the corner of her desk.

"Hi, may I help you find something?" she asked.

"I hope so," he said. He sounded worried.

The man was middle-aged with just a hint of gray hair starting at his temples. He was wearing a short-sleeved collared shirt in a muted plaid with navy pants and brown shoes. He looked to be somewhere in his mid to late forties, but his forehead had worry lines going across it and his blue eyes looked concerned.

"Well, let's give it a try," Lindsey said. She gave him a reassuring smile. "Tell me what you need."

"I grow roses," he said. "But I'm new to this area, and I'm not sure that my garden can survive the drought we're having. Do you have any books on growing roses specifically along the shoreline or in drought conditions?"

"Thanks to our local garden club, we have an excellent collection on that subject," Lindsey said. "I'll see what's available."

"Thank you," he said.

Lindsey searched the online catalog, limiting the results to the items that were currently available. She found three books on roses, but they weren't specific to the region. Still, they might have something in them about dealing with drought conditions. She noted the call numbers and then did a quick check of the local community webpages that they had bookmarked on the reference database by organization. She found several local gardening groups and one that specialized in roses. She swiveled the monitor on its base so her patron could see it.

"We do have some books in, but they aren't

specific to the area," she said. "However, there is a local rose club, and I am sure they can help you with your concerns about the current drought. Would you like me to write down their contact information for you?"

"Yes," he said. "Thank you. This is great."

Lindsey smiled. She took a piece of scratch paper and wrote down the name of the chapter president and her email address and phone number. She handed that to the man and then rose from her seat and said, "Let's go see what's on the shelves."

As she led him through the stacks of books, she asked, "So, you're new to Briar Creek?"

"Yes, my wife and I just moved here a few months ago," he said. "Just in time for me to plant a rose garden, but then this dry spell hit."

"It's a bad one," Lindsey said. "I've only been here for a few years myself, but the locals tell me that they've never seen anything like it."

"I hear the town is planning to ration water," he said. The lines in his forehead deepened.

"There has been some preparatory talk about that, Mr. . . . um, I'm sorry," Lindsey said. "I didn't introduce myself. I'm Lindsey Norris, the library director."

She held out her hand. The man stared at her and then her hand for a moment, and she wondered whether she had offended him.

"Aaron," he said. "Aaron Grady. It's nice to

meet you." He clasped her hand and gave it a firm squeeze before letting go.

Lindsey smiled and continued along the shelves until she reached the gardening section. She followed the Dewey Decimal numbers until she found books specifically about roses. The three books the online catalog had listed were there, as well as two more that she hadn't seen. She pulled them from the shelf and turned to find Mr. Grady right beside her. He was a bit too close, making her feel crowded, so she eased back a step. Instead of looking at the books she was holding, he was staring intently at her, with his hands down by his sides.

She'd had this sort of patron before, and they always amused her. They asked for books and she showed them the books, but when she took the books off the shelf, they didn't reach for them. They just stood there. Lindsey often wondered whether they thought she was planning to read the books to them. She usually broke the stalemate by forcibly pushing the books at them.

"Here you are," she said. She handed him the stack, keeping the most recently published book so that she could check the index. She flipped to the back and scanned for the word *drought*. The book referenced several pages on it, so she opened the book to those pages and skimmed the content. It listed different methods to maintain roses in a drought situation and even included a watering schedule. She handed Mr. Grady the open book and said, "This one looks like it will answer your question."

The lines that had been deepening on Mr. Grady's forehead eased and he gave her a closed-lip smile as he took the book and studied the pages.

"This is perfect," he said. "Thank you so much, Lindsey."

"You're welcome," she said. "Let me know how it goes, and if you have any more questions, I'm happy to help."

He smiled at her again, and Lindsey turned and headed back to the reference desk. She was relieved one of the books had answered Mr. Grady's questions. She always felt like it was a win when she could get a patron the answer they needed.

Back at the desk, she found Laura Hogan waiting for her. She was a tiny little thing but had the biggest heart in Briar Creek. She came in every week with her dog, Buck, and together they helped elementary school students who were struggling with learning how to read. Buck was a reading-therapy dog; essentially he sat on the floor with a student and listened while the child read aloud to him.

Buck was a beautiful black and brown dog with long legs and the softest ears Lindsey had ever felt. He was great friends with her dog,

Heathcliff, and the two of them cavorted and carried on when they met up at the dog park. As soon as Buck saw Lindsey, he started wagging his tail and let out a small whimper.

"Sorry, Buck," she said as she scratched his ears. "Heathcliff isn't here. It's just me." She glanced up at his human, who was smiling at her. "Hi, Laura, how are you?"

"Great, I'm looking forward to today's reading," she said. "We're halfway through *Gregor the Overlander*, and I can't wait to hear what happens next."

"The room is all set up," Lindsey said. "I'll just walk you over and unlock it for you."

"Thanks," Laura said. She patted her thigh, and Buck fell in beside her as they crossed the library to one of the study rooms. Lindsey unlocked the door and pushed it open.

"Lindsey!"

They both turned to see Mr. Grady hurrying toward them. Buck's ears went back and he growled low in his throat. Laura grabbed him by the collar and held him still.

"Weird," she said. "He's never done that before."

"He's likely more used to children," Lindsey said. She stepped forward and intercepted Mr. Grady so Buck wouldn't get more protective. "Yes, did you have another question?"

"Yes, actually," he said. He looked sheepish as

he clutched the rose books to his chest. "I don't have a library card. Is it possible for me to check out these books?"

"Absolutely," she said. "I'm sorry—I should have explained. To sign up for a card, we just need proof of your local residence, and then Ms. Cole at the circulation desk will sign you up and you'll be able to check out."

"I can do that," he said. He gave her a small smile and then backed away, watching her as he went.

Lindsey turned back to Laura and Buck. "Can I get you anything? Coffee? Water? Dog biscuit?"

"Coffee would be fantastic," Laura said. "But no treats for Buck, thanks. He's on a diet."

"Coming right up," Lindsey said.

She turned and headed for the staff break room. She grabbed a cup of coffee for Laura and a bowl of water for Buck. By the time those were delivered, her desk replacement, Ann Marie, had arrived, and Lindsey went to the back of the library, where her favorite activity, Thursday crafternoon, was held.

She brought her well-loved copy of *The House on Mango Street*, in which she'd stuck several sticky notes to mark the particularly pertinent passages she wanted to share. As she pushed open the door, she found that she was the last to arrive.

Beth was standing behind the table, dishing

out quesadillas, while Nancy Peyton and her best friend, Violet La Rue, were seated on the couch, holding full plates. Paula Turner, one of the circulation attendants, was pouring out the smoothies while Mary Murphy, Lindsey's soon-to-be sister-in-law, was standing with her baby, Josie, on her hip. Mary was swaying back and forth in her mama's stance while trying to eat. Lindsey headed right for her and held out her arms.

"I'll take her," she offered. Mary gave her a grateful look and handed off the baby.

"Thank you," she said. She studied Lindsey for a second, and then she grinned. "You look good with a baby in your arms."

Lindsey pressed her cheek to Josie's soft hair and laughed. "I said I'd hold her, not that I wanted any of my own."

"We'll see," Mary said. Then she grinned, a wide, warm smile just like her brother's, and sank into a nearby chair.

Lindsey moved around the room with Josie in her arms. A few months ago, she would have avoided holding her future niece as if she carried the plague. Lindsey wasn't really baby friendly, or she hadn't been until this kid came along. But Josie had the same sparkling blue eyes as her uncle, and her hair was already beginning to thicken into a cascade of dark curls just like his, and Lindsey had to admit she was smitten.

While Josie tugged on Lindsey's long blond curls, she joined Beth by the table and glanced at her friend. Beth had ditched her bat wings and the headband with the big ears. There was something about her that looked ethereal and lovely. She was watching Josie as if trying to understand the inner workings of her little mind.

Lindsey glanced from Beth to Josie and back. It occurred to her that she'd seen only one person glow like that before, and it was Mary when she was pregnant with Josie. Her eyes went wide, and she looked at Beth and said, "Oh my God, you're pregnant!"

She hadn't meant to say it so loud, and she cringed, aware that her guess could be wrong but also that Beth may not have wanted to share this news just yet. The entire room went quiet, and everyone turned to face them. Beth turned a deep shade of pink and then grinned. "How did you know? Am I showing already?" She hugged her belly. "Or is it my nose? Is it wider? I heard noses get bigger when a woman is pregnant."

"Another baby," Nancy said. She clapped her hands in delight. She tossed her gray bob, and her merry eyes twinkled as she turned to Violet and said, "You owe me five dollars."

Violet tutted. "That was a sucker's bet. We knew she'd get pregnant. I just thought it would be after summer."

A retired stage actress, Violet was still a great

beauty with dark skin, high cheekbones and a full and generous smile. She opened her purse and pulled out a five-dollar bill, which she slapped into Nancy's hand.

"You were betting on me?" Beth asked. She stared at the two women in amusement. "That is hilarious. What else are you two gambling about?"

Nancy and Violet both looked down at their food. As one they took bites of their quesadillas, and through a mouthful, Nancy mumbled, "Can't talk. Eating."

"Hmm-mmm-mm," Violet hummed in agreement.

Beth shook her head at them and then turned to Lindsey. "They are not fooling me one bit. You?"

"Not for a second," Lindsey said. She was about to question them when Nancy spoke first.

"Did you think the lead character, Esperanza, was aptly named?" Nancy asked.

"Yes, because it means *hope*," Violet said. "And her story is one of hoping for a better life."

Beth looked at Lindsey. "Those two are starting the book discussion instead of gossiping? They are definitely up to something."

"Agreed." Lindsey propped Josie on her hip and took a bite of the quesadilla Beth put on her plate. The tortilla had a little crunch, and stuffed with seasoned chicken and melted cheese and topped with *pico de gallo*, it was perfection.

20

She turned to Beth and said, "This is amazing."

"Thank you," Beth said. "Aidan's grandmother is from Mexico, and she's been teaching me how to make some of his favorites. He's better at it than I am, but I think I might have finally nailed the quesadilla."

"Yeah, you did," Mary said. This was no small praise, given that Mary owned the Blue Anchor, the only restaurant in town.

It was Paula who cracked the two older women. Having finished her lunch, she started to put out the craft supplies. While giving side-eye to Nancy and Violet, she asked, "So, if a library clerk wanted to get in on the action, what would she be betting on?"

Violet pointed to her mouth in a gesture that said she was still chewing. Nancy, having finished her food, was left to consider whether she should answer or not. The lure of having one more purse in the pot won.

"Nothing, really," she said with a shrug. She glanced at Ms. Cole, who had just arrived since she'd had to wait for another staff person to cover the circulation desk. "Do you ever gamble on silly things? You might want a piece of this."

"No," Ms. Cole said as she filled her plate. "Thank you."

Paula, who was Ms. Cole's assistant on the circulation desk, just smiled, clearly not surprised by her answer.

"We may have debated the possibility that Lindsey was going to elope for her wedding," Nancy said. She looked inquisitively at Lindsey. "So, care to tell us who owes whom a fiver?"

Josie grabbed a fistful of Lindsey's hair with her chubby fist and stuffed it into her mouth. She made a squinched-up face, which made Lindsey laugh because hair—ew.

"No, I don't. Did you know that author Sandra Cisneros is a Buddhist?" she asked the group.

Beth shook her head. "Nice try. There's no way you're going to change the subject on this one."

"I had to give it a go," Lindsey said.

Paula tossed her green braid over her shoulder. She was the hippest library staff member, with a sleeve of tattoos and colorful hair that she changed when the mood hit her. So far it had been purple and blue. Lindsey realized that if Paula ever went natural, she might not recognize her.

"Would you really elope, boss?" she asked Lindsey. "I mean, you only get married once."

"Statistically, that's not true," Ms. Cole said. When Beth gave her an exasperated look, Ms. Cole shrugged. "Fifty percent of marriages end in divorce."

"I'm not going to elope," Lindsey said. "In fact, my mom is coming to town in a few days, and we're going wedding-dress shopping. Also,

Sully and I are having a small ceremony on Bell Island in his parents' backyard."

"Oh," Nancy said. She looked cranky and slapped the five-dollar bill back into Vi's hand.

"Nancy!" Lindsey cried. Then she laughed. In truth, she would have bet she'd elope, too. Being an introvert, Lindsey wasn't really into the whole princess-for-a-day thing, and she was finding even the planning of a simple wedding to be a bit much.

"How small?" Nancy asked.

"Don't worry," Lindsey said. "You're all invited."

Josie made a hungry garble, and Mary immediately held up her arms. Lindsey handed over the baby, and they all moved to the craft table, where Paula had laid out the materials for this week's craft.

She'd put towels down on the table, and a tin can with water frozen inside of it was placed at each seat. Picking up an awl and a hammer, she demonstrated how to punch a hole in the can.

"Once they're finished and dry, you can paint them or not, then put a candle in them or tiny little battery lights. You can make a pattern or just punch random holes in them. The ice will keep the cans from denting while you tap in the holes, but you'll want to work fast so the ice doesn't melt, or you'll be sitting in a puddle."

The next few minutes were spent with everyone

punching holes in their cans. Lindsey, who was not crafty at all, discovered that there was a certain stress release to be found in tapping the awl through the metal to make a hole. She decided on a starburst pattern and was actually eager to see how it would come out when the ice melted. It occurred to her that these would make really cool centerpieces for her wedding.

She blinked. This was the first time she'd gotten excited about something for the wedding. Did this mean she was about to morph into a bridezilla? She scanned through all the things she had to do for the wedding. Nope. She still wasn't that jazzed about all the work involved. Okay, phew. Maybe she just liked punching holes in the can. It was rather therapeutic.

Her thoughts strayed to the book they'd read. She glanced around the table. The heroine in Cisneros's book wanted to escape Mango Street, her neighborhood in Chicago, and desperately longed for a house of her own. Lindsey glanced around the table and wondered whether all the women here felt the same way.

"What did you think about Esperanza's desire for her own home?" she asked.

"I thought it was very relatable," Nancy said. "When Jake and I bought our house, he insisted that the house be put in both of our names. He wanted to be sure it became mine in case anything happened to him. He was afraid one of his brothers would try to take the house, claiming I couldn't handle it by myself. Pfff."

She looked irritated for a moment and then sad, and Lindsey knew the memory of losing her captain husband when his boat went down during a storm haunted Nancy to this day.

"I was a single young woman in the early seventies, and while I didn't much care about owning a house, I did want to get a credit card in my own name," Violet said. "It wasn't allowed. Even though I was starring as the lead in a Broadway play, a woman had to have a husband to get a credit card. Huh. Now I have ten."

"I know what it's like to want to leave your past behind you," Paula said. "But I don't know that you really can. It shapes you, whether you like it or not. I think Esperanza learns that in the book. No matter how far she goes, Mango Street will always be part of her, even after she leaves."

"Sort of like Briar Creek and the Thumb Islands," Mary said. "I could travel anywhere in the world, but the years I've spent here have made me who I am. When I read the book, I realized how lucky I am to live here."

"I couldn't agree more," Ms. Cole said. She was tapping away on her tin can, and Lindsey glanced over to see the pattern she was making. It was the outline of an open book.

"That's brilliant," Lindsey said. She pointed to Ms. Cole's can, and the rest of the crafternooners took a look. As they heaped on the praise for her cleverness, Ms. Cole blushed a faint shade of pink. It looked pretty cute on her.

"Lindsey."

Lindsey glanced at the door to see Ann Marie there. She was holding a small piece of paper in her hand.

"This was left for you," Ann Marie said. She came into the room and handed Lindsey the note. "The patron wanted to give you the note himself, but I explained that you were at lunch."

"Oh, thanks," Lindsey said. She opened the note. In a small, tight script it read, *Lindsey, Thank you so much for your assistance today. I enjoyed our interaction and appreciate your help more than I can say. Fondly, Aaron Grady.*

"What does it say?" Ann Marie asked.

Lindsey glanced at her. "It's just a thank-you from Mr. Grady."

"The guy with the rose bushes," Ann Marie said. "He told me how your excellent research was going to save his precious roses."

"Well, that was thoughtful," Ms. Cole said.

"I don't know," Ann Marie said. "Maybe I'm paranoid because I read too many women-in-jeopardy thrillers, but I got a weird vibe off him."

"He seemed okay," Lindsey said. "A little socially awkward perhaps, but there's no harm in that. Right?"

"If you say so," Ann Marie said. With a wave, she exited the room.

"Looks like you have an admirer," Nancy said. She winked at Lindsey.

"What can I say?" Lindsey asked. "I give good reference."

"Wouldn't it be nice if all of our patrons took the time to write such nice notes?" Beth asked.

"Yes, because manners matter," Ms. Cole said. No one argued the point.

2

By the following week, the weather in Connecticut hadn't improved. The days were long and scorching hot. There had been no rain, and the normally lush green grass lawns in the center of town were now brittle, yellow and parched.

Lindsey left the town hall, which was just down the street from the library, wearing her summer business attire, which consisted of a sleeveless blue and white cotton gingham dress with white sandals. It was midafternoon, the sun was dialed to optimum bake, and there wasn't even a breeze blowing in from the bay, which was utterly flat, as if it didn't have the wherewithal to form a wave.

It wasn't a long walk, but by the time she reached the automatic doors of the library, she could feel the perspiration in her hair and running down her back. All she wanted was an ice-cold glass of water and a fan. She trudged into the building, knowing that her face was red and she was covered in perspiration.

She had almost reached the circulation desk when a voice called out, "Lindsey!"

She thought about ignoring the person and just going for the water cooler, but the manners her parents had instilled in her wouldn't let her. She pushed a heavy hank of hair out of her face and turned around.

"I brought you these." Mr. Grady, the patron she had helped several days before, was standing there with a batch of roses.

Lindsey blinked, feeling a little woozy from the overpowering smell of the roses combined with what she was beginning to think was a mild case of heat stroke. Still, as Ms. Cole had said, manners mattered, and she said, "Thank you, Mr. Grady. They're lovely."

"Call me Aaron," he said.

"Okay," she said. But she didn't say his name. Maybe the heat was making her feel contrary, or perhaps it was that his presence was becoming an impediment to her getting water, but she just nodded. She took the flowers and put them on the far side of the return desk. "If you'll excuse me, I have to go."

She let her voice trail off, and she staggered into the workroom where the water cooler was. She poured herself a glass and downed half of it, then pressed the cup she had used against her cheek, as if she could lower her body temperature from the outside.

"You look like you're going to pass out," Ms. Cole said as she came into the workroom.

She grabbed a paper towel and doused it with cold water. "Put this around your neck, and go sit down before you fall down."

"Thank you," Lindsey said. She filled her cup again and went into her office, where she put the free-standing fan on high and let it blast her with its breezy goodness.

Ms. Cole watched from the door. When Lindsey sat down, she said, "Mr. Grady arrived shortly after you left and has been waiting for you."

"Oh, I'm sorry if I was rude to him, but it's just so hot out there," Lindsey said. She made to rise, and Ms. Cole waved her back down.

"No, you were fine," she said. "You were clearly overheated. We're having record heat today. If anything, he was rude to detain you when you were clearly about to faint."

Lindsey drank more water. She could feel Ms. Cole staring at her. "What's the matter?"

"I think Ann Marie might have been right about him," Ms. Cole said. "There's something off about that man."

"Has he done anything specific that makes you think he might cause harm to the staff or the library?" Lindsey asked. She was finally feeling a bit cooler now, and she could feel her brain kicking into library-director mode.

"Not the staff or the library," Ms. Cole said. "To be honest, he seems fixated on you."

"Me?" Lindsey asked. "But why?"

"I don't know," Ms. Cole said. "But he waited here for two hours, and every chance he got, he tried to engage the staff in conversation about you."

Lindsey felt her stomach drop. She was already nauseated from the heat. This did not help. "What did he want to know?"

"All sorts of things," Ms. Cole said. "What your favorite color is, where do you live, do you have any hobbies, that sort of thing."

Lindsey pressed a hand to her forehead. "Okay, that is weird."

"No one told him anything, of course," Ms. Cole said. "And Beth was very clear that it was inappropriate of him to be asking about you."

"Good," Lindsey said. "How did he respond to that?"

"He completely ignored her," Ms. Cole said. "I think you're going to have to be very firm with him."

"Okay," Lindsey said. "Thanks for the heads-up. Maybe it was a good thing I was on the verge of passing out when I arrived."

"Just . . ." Ms. Cole paused and then said, "Be careful."

Lindsey watched her leave and wondered what that was about. She didn't know a lot about Ms. Cole's past. She had been born and raised in Briar Creek, and as far as Lindsey knew, she had never married or had children. Presently, she was dating Milton Duffy, library board president, yogi and town historian, but other than that, Lindsey didn't know much. She wondered what made Ms. Cole look as nervous as she did about this situation. She knew it was none of her business, but she'd become quite fond of Ms. Cole, and she didn't like the thought that somewhere in her past lurked a terrible hurt.

She supposed she could go talk to Mr. Grady and make it clear that she was unavailable and that while she appreciated the roses, she thought they were inappropriate. She felt a trickle of sweat run down her back. Ugh, or she could just wait until she saw him again. Maybe he was just a lonely guy in a new town and she was the first friendly person he'd met. Not being a huge fan of confrontation, Lindsey sincerely hoped this was the case and opted to stay in her office until she felt like she wasn't going to throw up.

Heather Cooper, one of Lindsey's favorite patrons, was visiting the library with her husband, Brett. They were checking out a bunch of travel books for an upcoming trip to Disneyland. Heather was Lindsey's go-to source for horror books and cozy mysteries, and they always had a nice long chat about the books they were enjoying.

"At least you'll be escaping this drought," Lindsey said. "Think of us when you're riding Pirates of the Caribbean."

"Meh, I'm originally from Arizona," Heather said. She tossed her long light brown hair over her shoulder and pushed her glasses up on her nose. "This is nothing. And Brett's from Australia, so he's seen worse, too."

"I can't even imagine," Lindsey said. She dreaded the thought of going out in the heat, but at least she was closing the library and it would be after dark with no more scorching sun when she left work.

After Heather and Brett checked out their materials, the staff checked the building and began locking up. When they stepped through the back door, the heat was like a punch to the face.

The drought continued with no rain in the forecast, and it was making everyone cranky and irritable, including Lindsey. She was on her bike tonight since Sully had an evening boat tour scheduled. He told her the only good things about being out on the water were that he could make his own breeze with the speed of the boat and that the splash from the waves actually cooled things down. Lindsey envied him that right now. As she dropped her book bag into the basket on her bicycle, she dreaded the sticky ride home.

The summer sun was finally setting, and once she got the bike up to speed, the air did feel good against her slick skin. She took a shortcut through town to the gray shingled beach house she shared with Sully near the shore. Her dog, Heathcliff, would be waiting for her, and she couldn't wait to take him to the beach for his nightly walk. She might even go for a swim in the ocean just to cool off.

She turned onto their road, which ran along the shore. The houses were small, but the yards were big. Sand dusted the pothole-marked road, but she had ridden this route enough to know exactly where to swerve even in the dimming light. She rode up to the deck that surrounded the house and parked her bike beside the stairs. She could hear Heathcliff barking, and she quickly locked her bike to the rail and grabbed her book bag.

She hurried up the steps, eager to get out of the heat. She unlocked the door and strode into the house. She had just enough time to drop her bag and brace her legs before he saw her. Heathcliff let out a delighted yip and ran full speed for her, launching himself at her and nearly knocking her to the floor.

"Easy, fella," she said. She rubbed his sides and his ears and noted that his tongue was hanging out as if he, too, was suffering from the heat. His furry black body was all aquiver, and he used his front paws to hug her leg, a habit he had that melted Lindsey's heart every time. She bent down and hugged him back.

"Just let me change, and we'll go for a walk," she said. Heathcliff pranced, clearly fully aware of what the word *walk* meant.

She flicked on the living room light and strode down the hall to her bedroom. She shucked off her work clothes and pulled on her bathing suit. Then she grabbed an old T-shirt of Sully's and pulled it over her head.

She was about to grab a towel out of the linen closet when there was a knock on the door. Heathcliff barked, letting whoever was at the door know he was there. Heathcliff was a total mama's boy and took his job protecting Lindsey very seriously.

She walked back to the front door, patting Heathcliff on the way. "It's all right," she said. "You can stand down for the moment."

He sat, but he kept growling a low menacing rumble that was accompanied by one of his furry black eyebrows being raised as if he was suspicious of whoever was knocking. It hit Lindsey, as it often did, how much she loved this dog. She patted him again and turned to the door.

She glanced through the window beside the door to see who it was. She felt her heart sink into her feet. It was Aaron Grady, holding another enormous bouquet of roses.

3

Lindsey debated pretending she wasn't home. She didn't want to answer the door in her bathing suit, even with a shirt over it, to anyone, never mind a stranger. And she really didn't want to have a library patron standing on her doorstep. Yes, Briar Creek was a small town and everyone knew everyone, but there were still boundaries that needed to be maintained—and not showing up at her house uninvited late in the day was one of them.

For that matter, how did Grady know where she lived? Had he followed her home? She knew her staff wouldn't have given out her personal information, but maybe he had asked someone in town. Since she lived with Sully and the house was in his name only, her address wasn't publicly available. She felt her inner alarm system go off like a high-pitched siren. She grabbed her phone and called Beth.

"Hey, Lindsey," Beth answered on the second ring. "What's up?"

"The patron that Ann Marie got the weird vibe about? He's standing at my front door, holding another vase full of roses," she said.

37

"Oh no, do not open that door," Beth said. "Where's Sully?"

"Giving an evening boat tour around the islands," Lindsey said.

"I'll send Aidan over. He can be there in ten minutes," Beth said. "Ann Marie was right. The guy is a weirdo."

"I'm going to explain to him why this is bad," Lindsey said. "But I want you on the line just in case."

"Don't," Beth cried. "Seriously, he'll go away if you don't answer."

"Yes, but I need to make it perfectly clear that this is unacceptable," Lindsey said.

"I wish Sully was there," Beth said. Then she gasped. "Do you think he waited until he knew you were alone?"

Uneasiness rippled through Lindsey. Had he? That was even creepier than she'd been thinking. She could hear Beth talking to someone, presumably Aidan, in the background. Ugh, she hated being put in this position, but there was no doubt that Grady was crossing a line.

"Just stay on the phone, okay?" Lindsey asked.

"Sure, but Aidan and I are on our way," Beth said. She was huffing and puffing, and Lindsey could tell she was running.

"I don't think that's necessary, but okay," Lindsey said. She knew telling Beth not to come wasn't an option. In truth, she'd do the exact same thing.

There was another sharp knock on the door. Lindsey drew in a steadying breath and opened the door just a crack. She peered out with the phone visible at her ear. Then she said, "Hold on, I have someone at the door." She glanced at Grady without smiling and said, "Yes?"

Grady's eyes shifted from side to side. He licked his lips, looking nervous. Lindsey hoped he was feeling as uncomfortable as she was.

"I brought these for you," he said. He thrust the bouquet of roses at her. In the heat the smell of the blooms was a bit overpowering. Lindsey didn't take them.

"I'll just put them down," he said. He looked so earnest, like a kid offering a fistful of wild-flowers to his mom. "I picked them just for you as a thank-you for helping me and because you seemed to like the ones I brought to the library. I thought you'd like some at your home, too."

Grady was in his usual pressed pants and button-down shirt. If he were in a lineup, he'd look like the feckless accountant thrown in just to have another body present. Was he really so socially inept that he thought finding out where a woman lived and bringing her flowers at night was okay? It wasn't. It made Lindsey feel vulnerable in ways she didn't like, and she wasn't doing him any favors by playing nice and letting him think it was all right. If he did this to someone else, he could get a black eye or worse.

"Mr. Grady, this is very inappropriate," Lindsey said. "I don't know how you found out where I live, but showing up at my house uninvited is not okay. Please leave."

Grady's eyes went wide, as if he hadn't even considered the possibility that what he was doing was impolite. His face turned pink and then red and then pale. He looked mortified.

"I . . . oh . . . I am so sorry," he mumbled. "I didn't . . . I would never . . ."

Heathcliff pressed up against Lindsey's leg. He growled low in his throat, the sound carrying through the crack in the door and out into the night. Grady's eyes widened in alarm. So now she and her dog had embarrassed and scared him.

Having been an introvert most of her life, Lindsey felt a pang of sympathy for him. Clearly, he hadn't thought his gesture of gratitude through. She felt her shoulders drop and she tried to soften her words.

"Listen, I appreciate the gesture, but you can't just show up at my house," she said.

"Oh, but I thought we connected," he said. He gestured between them. "I thought you were my friend."

He had a little-boy-lost look about him that, again, made Lindsey feel unduly harsh, but she felt as if she had to be clear; otherwise he might think he could show up here whenever he liked, and that wouldn't do. This was her sanctuary away from work and people and life. She was a solitary person. She wasn't even on any social media, preferring books as her escape, and she guarded her privacy fiercely.

"No, we're not friends," she said. "I am a librarian and you are a patron. That's as far as it goes."

"Yes, of course," he said. He didn't make eye contact with her. He bobbed his head and stepped back across the porch and down the steps.

"Don't forget your roses," Lindsey said.

Heathcliff continued to growl.

Grady glanced at her quickly and then away. "Please keep them as an apology. I'm sorry to have interrupted your evening."

Lindsey was about to tell him it was all right when she noticed he had lowered his gaze to her body and was staring at her in a way that made her distinctly uncomfortable. She stepped quickly behind the door so that only her face was visible.

"Good night, Mr. Grady," she said.

"Good night, Ms. Norris," he said. He turned and hurried to a silver sedan parked on the street in front of her house. Lindsey took note of the license plate just in case.

As his car shot down the road, it passed a pickup truck coming in the opposite direction. Lindsey felt the tension in her ease as she recognized Beth and Aidan. A part of her felt ridiculous to be so unnerved by a library patron who appeared to be trying to be nice, but as Ms. Cole and the others had noted, there was something off about Aaron Grady.

The truck parked in the drive, and Beth and Aidan popped out. Aidan stood behind the open driver's-side door and asked, "Was that him? Should I go after him and knock him around a bit?"

Beth looked at her husband with adoration, and Lindsey was grateful for the offer, too, but like Beth, Aidan was a children's librarian, and she knew he didn't have the sort of personality to rough up a stranger. Besides, it would have the potential to destroy his career.

"I really appreciate the offer, but I think I made my feelings known to him," Lindsey said. "I don't think Mr. Grady will be bothering me anymore."

Beth held up her phone as she crossed the yard to Lindsey. "You were great, but people like him, who get fixated on a person, don't always hear what you say. You're going to have to keep your guard up."

"I will," Lindsey said. "I promise."

She noticed that both Beth and Aidan looked hot, and she said, "I was just about to take Heathcliff for a walk on the beach. Want to come?"

"That sounds lovely," Beth said. "How about you, honey?"

"Count me in," Aidan agreed. "Not for nothing, but I think we should stick around until Sully gets home, just to be on the safe side."

Lindsey was about to protest but then thought better of it and said, "Thanks. I really appreciate it."

She opened the door to let Beth and Aidan in, much to Heathcliff's tail-wagging, knee-hugging delight. She glanced down at the vase of flowers. She didn't pick them up.

Sully arrived home before they were back from their walk on the beach, and Lindsey let them into the house to find him in the kitchen. The roses were sitting on the counter. Lindsey picked them up and put them back outside while Beth and Aidan greeted Sully.

Sully watched her with his eyebrows raised. "Is there a reason those are supposed to be outside?"

"Yes, they came from a creepy patron," she said.

"Oh?" He looked like he wanted the rest of the story.

"And on that note, we'll head out and let you two talk," Aidan said. He took Beth's hand and steered her toward the door. "If you need us, call us."

Beth paused beside Lindsey to give her a hug.

"It'll be okay. You were very firm. I bet he gets the message now."

"Let's hope," Lindsey said. She closed the door after them and locked it.

She turned to find Sully rubbing Heathcliff's belly. Her man and her dog. She never got tired of watching the mutual affection between them.

"Creepy patron, huh?" he asked.

"Yeah," she said. "I'm sure it's nothing, but I helped him a few days ago with a reference request about maintaining his roses during this drought, and he brought me some roses at work as a thank-you."

"That seems nice," he said.

"It was," she agreed. "Until he showed up at the house tonight with those." She pointed at the door with her thumb.

He frowned. "How did he know where you live?"

"Exactly," she said. "So I explained to him that there were boundaries and he was crossing them. He said he just wants to be my friend, but I said no, that I was just a librarian and he shouldn't do anything like this again."

Sully blew out a breath and put a hand on the back of his neck. "Do you think he understood?"

"I hope so," she said. "I mean, if he asked someone about me and where I live, I'm certain they would mention that I'm marrying you. Plus, when I first helped him, he said he was married,

44

so it could be that he really does just want to be friends, but it feels weird and awkward and I don't like it."

Sully opened his arms, and Lindsey stepped into them. He rested his cheek on her head, and she felt herself relax against him. It wasn't that she expected Sully to fight her battles for her, but it felt good to have him here with her, a solid presence against the vulnerability she was feeling.

"Do you want me to talk to him?" Sully asked. "I can be very persuasive."

Lindsey leaned back and met his bright blue gaze. A former navy man, he owned a tour-boat and water-taxi company servicing the islands in the bay. He was tall and broad with a sailor's build, and his calloused hands and suntanned skin marked him as a man of the outdoors. Despite Grady's love of gardening, he stood no chance against a man like Sully.

"No, I really think he heard me tonight," she said. "I was very clear that showing up at the house was inappropriate. I can't imagine that he would persist after that."

"Tell you what—Charlie is helping out with the tours over the summer, so that frees me up to be your chauffeur," he said. "I'll do drop-off and pickup duty with you until we're sure that this guy isn't a problem."

"I don't want to put you out," she said.

"Don't worry about it. Charlie needs the money. His band broke up again."

"Poor Charlie," Lindsey said.

Charlie Peyton was Nancy's nephew, and when Lindsey had rented an apartment from Nancy in her three-family house, Charlie had lived in the apartment between them, like the peanut butter holding together the bread in the sandwich. He'd been a delightful neighbor, except during band practice. Lindsey still wasn't sure her hearing had recovered.

"Yeah, he's pretty bummed out, but the extra work will keep him from overthinking it."

"All right," she said. "I've read enough crime novels to know to err on the side of caution."

"That's my girl," he said. He let her go and reached for his water bottle on the counter. He gave her side-eye when he asked, "What did you say his name was again?"

"I didn't," she said.

He grimaced as if he'd been hoping to slip that by her. Lindsey smiled.

"His name is Aaron Grady, and he just moved to Briar Creek a few months ago," she said. "All I know about him is he loves his roses."

"What are you going to do if he disregards what you said and brings you more flowers?" Sully asked.

"I don't know," she said. "I mean, he's creepy, but he doesn't say anything inappropriate or threatening. I'm not really sure why he's bringing me flowers. Do you think I'm overreacting?"

"Did it make you feel weird when he was at the door?" Sully asked.

"Yes."

"Then you're not overreacting," he said. "Always trust your instincts. I learned that in the navy. If something didn't feel right in my gut, ninety-nine times out of a hundred, my gut was right."

"And it's weird, right?" she asked. "Showing up at someone's house when you hardly know them? I mean, what did he think was going to happen? We were going to hang out and be besties?"

"I'm pretty sure that's not what he was thinking," Sully said. Lindsey gave him an *Ew* face, and he shrugged. "Let's just be hyper-vigilant for a while, okay?"

"Okay." Lindsey sighed. How had she gotten here? She was just doing her job as a reference provider. Why did it have to get weird?

For three days, Lindsey watched the front doors of the library, tensing if she thought Grady was entering the building. Usually, it was just another man with pressed pants and a short-sleeved dress shirt. On the third day, she finally felt as if she could relax her guard. Clearly, her message had gotten through to him. She felt the teensiest pang of guilt that perhaps she'd been rude, but then she remembered that the guy had shown up at her house, late in the evening, and she still had no idea how he had discovered where she lived.

That alone checked any worries she had that she'd been uncivil. She didn't know him. He didn't know her. And this notion that he thought they could be friends made her uncomfortable. Friendship wasn't something that switched on and off like a light switch. Friendships took years to develop, requiring time spent together and secrets shared and trust built. It wasn't something that happened because a librarian helped you find some books.

Sure, Lindsey had patrons who had become friends, but it had taken months and sometimes years for those relationships to form. Despite what Grady said, she couldn't shake the feeling that his interest in her was inappropriate at best and downright creepy at worst.

Luckily, she was now off for a long weekend and could put some distance between herself and the awkwardness. She dreaded having Grady show up at the library, as she wasn't really sure how to treat him. She was leery of being too friendly but didn't want to be unduly harsh either.

Her weekend started with the arrival of her parents in Briar Creek and a cookout at the house with Sully making his famed barbecue ribs. From there, her parents went to stay on Bell Island with Sully's parents in a getting-to-know-you parental weekend that she was certain would make the four of them as close as in-laws could be.

And now Lindsey's mom and Sully's mom were with her and Beth while they went wedding-dress shopping in New Haven. Lindsey had left her entourage in the lounge outside the dressing room while she tried on gowns. While she appreciated the help, there was a large part of her that would have preferred to be out fishing with her dad, Sully and his father. Still, immersed in all of these very normal pre-wedding events, it made Lindsey feel as if she could put "the Grady Incident," as she had begun to think of it, behind her.

Being medium in build in both height and shape, Lindsey wasn't sure what dress would make the most of her average assets. Because the wedding would be in December, she needed to find a dress quickly if there were going to be any alterations required. She wished she was the type of woman who'd had her wedding planned from the day she was five years old. She was not.

Lindsey's life had been lived in the pages of books. In that regard, she'd been married a thousand times, in every possible ceremony and every possible bridal gown, from outer space to a fantasy wedding where she was a Druid bride, all the way through history to a modern-day wedding where the bride was actually in love with the groom's brother. Drama! Truly, within the pages of books, she had the wedding thing down. In real life, not so much, as evidenced by the fact that she was in yet another fitting room in yet another bridal salon, trying on yet another mountain of dresses, none of which said, *Pick me. Choose me. I am your dress.*

"Arms up," Diane, the petite owner of the shop, ordered.

Lindsey did as she was told, and Diane dropped the silky confection down over her head. As Diane fussed to make it hang just right, Lindsey hesitated to look in the mirror. She was reaching the end of her patience with trying on gowns, and she wanted very badly to feel like this was *the one.*

"Okay, what do you think?" Diane asked. She spun Lindsey around to face the mirror. Lindsey blinked. *Oh.* The dress was exquisite. A fitted gown of pale blue was just visible beneath the sheer white lace dress that floated over it. The cut of the gown flattered her figure, and the long sleeved lace was perfect for a winter wedding. All of the details were lovely, but it was how the dress made her feel that did the trick. This was the first dress Lindsey had tried on that made her feel like a bride.

"If winter comes early, the blue beneath the lace will look amazing against a snowy background." Diane considered Lindsey in the mirror. "Will you wear your hair up or down?"

"Down," Lindsey said. "But maybe pulled back?"

"Let's see," Diane said. She plucked two hair combs from her apron pocket and twisted up half of Lindsey's hair, fixing it in place with the combs. "Yes, I'd definitely consider a half-up, half-down if I were you."

She was right. It was only the second dress Lindsey had tried on in this shop, but it was definitely the one that got her vote.

"Come out already," Beth called into the dressing room. "We're *dying* out here."

This was their third stop of the day, Diane's Bridal, a tiny dress shop in central New Haven. It was located on the first floor of an old redbrick building that used to be a button factory. The wood floors were polished to a high gloss, and big bay windows looked out onto the street.

Lindsey pushed back the curtain of the dressing room and strode out into the main room, with the full pale blue skirt and lace overlay billowing around her. There was a gasp, and she looked up to see both Sully's mother, Joan, and her mom, Christine, clasping their hands together and smiling. Beth, being the most exuberant of them all, was bouncing up and down on her feet as if she couldn't contain her excitement.

"You are stunning! That's the one!" she declared. She looked at the moms. "Don't you think? That's the one?"

The moms looked at each other, and then Lindsey's mom spoke. "It depends on whether it's the one Lindsey wants. Is it, dear?"

Lindsey picked up her skirts and climbed the steps to stand on the dais with the three mirrors. She checked her reflection from every angle. She turned around and faced them. "I think we have a winner."

"Yes!" Joan clapped. "My goodness, Sully is going to keel over when he sees you in that."

Lindsey laughed. "So long as he bounces right back up again."

"Oh, honey," Christine said. "You are going to be such a beautiful bride."

A tear slid down her cheek, and Lindsey reached forward and hugged her mom. She was shorter than Lindsey, and her blond hair had lightened to white in recent years, but they shared the same hazel eyes, wide smile, stubborn chin and somewhat prominent nose. When she looked at her mom, she could see herself in the future, and it hit her that like her mom had had her dad by her side for most of her life, Lindsey would now have Sully. The thought made her smile.

She looked at her mom with a bit of wonder and said, "I'm getting married."

Christine laughed and hugged her close. Lindsey knew at that moment that all the things she'd been worried about in regards to the wedding just didn't matter. The only thing that mattered was that at the end of it, Sully would be her husband.

She turned to see Diane standing in the doorway to the fitting room and said, "I'll take it."

After a grueling morning of dress shopping, the ladies agreed that only a pizza at New Haven's Wooster Square would do, so they set out to enjoy a ladies' lunch, which included a brick oven–baked white clam pie. Heaven.

It struck Lindsey as she and Beth listened to Joan and Christine reflect upon their marriages, both of which were approaching forty-year anniversaries, that while it was true that both Joan and Christine had chosen their mates wisely, there was also a level of stick-to-it-ness that was required for a marriage to survive.

Lindsey knew that her mom had to endure her father's snoring; truly, he was a champ and hit decibels that other snorers only dreamed of. She hadn't known until today that her mom had devised a system in which she sandwiched her head in between two pillows to drown out the noise. Joan shared that Sully's father suffered from an acute case of male refrigerator blindness. Not a day passed that he didn't stand in front of the open refrigerator and ask her where something was that was usually right in front of him. Beth glanced between the two of them as if taking notes.

Lindsey looked at her and said, "Nothing to report about Aidan?"

Beth glanced around the table with a worried expression. She bit her lip and said, "Well, we have had some discussions . . ."

"About?" Lindsey asked.

"Video games," Beth said.

Joan and Christine both raised their eyebrows, and Lindsey knew this was likely a generational problem. She'd seen both Sully and Aidan get that glazed look in their eyes when Beth and Aidan came over for dinner and the two men busted out Sully's gaming console. While she and Beth were happy to take them on in a tournament of *Super Smash Bros.*, Sully and Aidan had the stamina to play *Black Ops II* into the night for hours.

"Since we found out that I'm pregnant, he gets up in the middle of the night and plays video games," she said. "He says it relaxes him, but I'm afraid he's doing it because he's afraid that once the baby comes, he won't have any time to himself anymore." She was quiet for a moment. "We argued about it."

Joan smiled. She tucked her silver hair behind her ear and reached across the table to pat Beth's hand. "When I was pregnant, Mike used to go out night fishing. Scared the living daylights out of me, thinking he was going to fall asleep and fall in the water and drown."

54

"When I was pregnant with Lindsey and her brother, Jack, John used to get up and graph sentences and study the derivation of words," Christine said. She looked at Lindsey. "Always the professor of etymology."

"So this is normal?" Beth asked.

"Absolutely," Joan said.

"Fatherhood is a big wake-up call for a man," Christine said. "Even though times have changed and women contribute to the household income just as much, and frequently more, than men, they still have that be-the-provider thing. I think it freaks them out."

"Oh, phew." Beth collapsed back into her chair. "I was afraid deep down he was changing his mind about the whole parenting thing." She gestured at her still-slim belly. "Too late."

They all laughed, and Lindsey heard the notification chime from her phone. She wondered whether it was Sully reporting in from his fishing trip. Suddenly, she missed him with an intensity that was almost painful.

"Excuse me," she said. She reached down into her bag and picked up her phone. She thumbed it open and glanced at the text icon. It indicated a new message, so she opened it. The number wasn't one she recognized, and she assumed it was an advertisement. It wasn't.

The message read, *I liked you in the first dress. Choose that one for me.*

4

A chill ran through her, and Lindsey's head
snapped up from her phone as she scanned
the restaurant. Anyone she knew who would
text her about her dress would be in her phone.
Her brother, Jack, was the only one who would
send her a text from an unrecognizable number,
because Jack lived an adventurous life by the
seat of his pants, but the last she'd heard he was
in Boston, behaving himself. Still.

"Mom, did you text Dad or Jack about my
dress?" she asked.

"No, I thought you'd want to do that," she said.
She smiled at Lindsey but then frowned. "Are
you all right, dear? You look pale."

"I'm fine." Lindsey forced herself to smile. She
was as far from fine as completely freaked out
could possibly be, but she was not about to let her
mother know. "I'm just worn out from trying on
so many dresses." She looked at Joan and Beth.
They were her only hope for the weirdness not to
be so weird. She asked, "You didn't text anyone
about the dress, did you?"

"No," Joan said. "I don't want Sully to get a
glimpse until the day of your wedding."

"Nope," Beth said. Her eyes narrowed as she took in the expression on Lindsey's face. "Why?"

Lindsey shook her head. "I just got a text about wedding dresses from a number I don't recognize. It's probably nothing."

Joan turned to Christine and said, "Those telemarketers can find you anywhere, I swear."

"I know," Christine agreed. "I looked online for a new dishwasher, and the next thing I knew, ads for dishwashers were popping up all over the place."

"It's very creepy," Joan agreed. "And pushy."

"Excuse me," Beth said. "I need to use the restroom. Lindsey, don't you need to go, too?"

"No," Lindsey said. One look at Beth's face and she knew she was going to the restroom. "Oh, wait—yeah, I do. Excuse us."

Together they cut through the restaurant of red and white checked linen tables and empty Chianti bottles hanging from the ceiling. Once they got into the bathroom, Beth turned on her.

"What happened?"

"Noth—"

Beth shook her head. Lindsey sighed and held out her phone. Beth read the text, and her eyes went wide.

"It's him, isn't it?" she asked. "That creep, Grady."

Lindsey shrugged. "I don't know, but I can't

imagine who else in my life would send something like this."

Beth handed Lindsey her phone and went over to the sink and started washing her hands. "I feel like I'm contaminated just by reading that. What does that even mean? 'Choose it for me'? Ish."

"I have no idea," Lindsey said. She pocketed her phone and washed her hands, too. "I'm going to take it to Emma and see what she thinks."

"Good idea," Beth said. "How about this afternoon?"

"I can't," Lindsey said. "Once we get back to Briar Creek, I'm going with Mom and Joan out to Bell Island to join the men for dinner. Sully is picking us up."

"He'd want you to tell Emma," Beth said.

"And I will, first thing in the morning," Lindsey said.

Beth stared at her.

"I promise."

"Swear on your perfect wedding dress," Beth said. She took these things very seriously.

Lindsey laughed. "I swear on my perfect wedding dress."

Sully and Heathcliff were waiting for them at the pier when they arrived back in Briar Creek in the midafternoon. The sun shone on Sully's reddish-brown curls, and his blue eyes crinkled in the corners when he saw her. He opened his arms wide, but Heathcliff ran around him to get to Lindsey first. He launched his furry black body at her, and Lindsey just had time to brace herself as Heathcliff hit her with all thirty-five pounds of wiggling dog. Lindsey bent down and gave him an all-over body rub.

When she straightened back up, Sully was watching them with a grin, and he opened his arms and gave her a solid hug. Back with her boys, it was the best Lindsey had felt since reading the worrisome text.

"Success?" Sully asked.

"And how," she said. She smiled at him. "Check *find a dress* off the to-do list."

"Fantastic," he said. "We're one step closer to being wife and husband and dog."

Lindsey laughed. Being near him made the boogeyman go away; suddenly the creepy text just seemed stupid and silly and not worth ruining her day over.

"All aboard," Sully called. He led the way to where his water taxi was docked, and he handed each of them into the boat.

The moms, as Lindsey was beginning to think of them, took the bench seat at the back of the boat while she took the seat beside Sully's. He pushed off the pier and jumped into the boat. He started up the engine, and Lindsey felt herself relax. She was glad they were going to be on the island for the evening; putting some distance between herself and the town might make her feel better.

Heathcliff bounded up onto the bow, his preferred spot, and he wagged and barked at the waves they puttered through. They were in the no-wake zone, so the boat moved slowly, maneuvering around the rocks hidden just below the water's surface.

They were almost out of sight of the pier when Lindsey felt the hair on the back of her neck prickle. She thought maybe it was the cooler breeze on the water after the hot air inland, but an intuition or instinct compelled her to look back at the dock. Standing at the end of the pier, watching their boat, stood Aaron Grady.

While she stared at him in horror, he raised his arm and waved. Lindsey knew without a doubt that he was the one who had texted. He was watching her, following her, stalking her. She thought she might throw up.

As if he sensed something was wrong, Sully glanced from Lindsey to where she stared. He frowned. Over the sound of the motor, he shouted, "Is that him? The rose guy?"

Lindsey nodded. Sully's face went dark, as if he was seriously debating turning the boat around to go confront Grady. Lindsey stepped close to him, not wanting the moms to hear.

"He followed me today," she said. "He watched me try on dresses."

"What the he—" he began, but Lindsey interrupted.

"Shh," she said. "I don't want to alarm the moms."

Sully's features were tight, but he gave her a quick nod. Quietly, he said, "This ends tonight. When we go home, we're going to talk to Emma on the way."

"Agreed," Lindsey said. Then she put her arm around him. She could feel the tension in his bunched-up shoulders. "Hey, relax. It'll be okay." His shoulders remained taut. Lindsey wrapped her arms around him while he increased the speed of the boat as if he wanted to get her out of there. "Do I have to hug it out of you?"

At that, she felt the tension in him ease. He steered with one hand while putting his calloused hand over hers as if he could keep her close and protect her.

"That might help," he said. He turned his head and kissed her quick. "I hate that this guy is doing this. It makes me want to punch something—him."

"I know," she said. "But don't. I need you."

"Don't worry," he said. "You've got me, one hundred percent."

Bell Island was one of the largest of the Thumb Islands. It had all the perks, electricity and plumbing, and several families lived on the island year-round, unlike the smaller islands that were mostly summer homes. Sully and his younger sister, Mary, had grown up on the island. Since then, a few of the families had changed, but the island remained the same.

When Sully had mentioned to Lindsey that he'd always thought he'd get married on the island, she had been all in. They agreed that it would be a simple civil ceremony with just their closest friends and family in attendance. Lindsey was pretty sure they could handle that. Mike and Joan Sullivan's house on Bell Island had a large yard, and Joan was a gardener, so it was a beautiful space eight months out of the year, before the winter snow hit, which was beautiful, too, in its own way.

The men had been successful in their fishing, and they ate a hearty meal of grilled sea bass and red potatoes under festive paper lanterns hanging across the backyard. Mary and her husband, Ian, had ditched their duties as restaurant proprietors for the night to join them for dinner. Lindsey was grateful as Ian managed to jolly the worried expression off Sully's face.

While Joan and Christine whipped up a dessert of strawberry shortcake in the kitchen, Lindsey and Mary sprawled on a blanket watching baby Josie crawl in the grass with Heathcliff at her side. The men lounged on the deck overlooking the water to enjoy their cigars downwind of the rest of them.

"If I knew my brother less well than I do, I might not notice that he's been watching you all night," Mary said. "And while he's clearly smitten, this is more of a worried look. What's going on?"

Lindsey debated not telling her future sister-in-law. She really didn't want a fuss. But then, she knew that the situation with Grady was probably going to come out anyway, and perhaps having as many eyes on her problem as the town could muster wouldn't be such a bad thing. She gave Mary the short version. It didn't make it any less weird or creepy, and judging by Mary's face, she wasn't assured that it was nothing.

"Listen, I can tell you're embarrassed by this, but you shouldn't be," Mary said. "You didn't do anything wrong."

"I know—I do—but I just keep thinking I should have handled the whole thing differently, and then I wouldn't be dealing with this mess," Lindsey said.

"No, this isn't on you," Mary said. She reached across the blanket to scoop up Josie, who had grabbed a dandelion and was about to shove it into her mouth. She took the flower and then did a magical switcheroo with one of Josie's wooden blocks. Josie grasped the wooden block in her chubby fists, completely distracted.

Mary looked back at Lindsey and said, "Before I met Ian, I was working in New Haven as a bartender. One night after closing, one of my coworkers followed me home. He pushed his way into my apartment and—"

Her voice broke, and Lindsey studied her friend's face. The look of pain etched there made her stomach knot. The sweat from the warm evening felt clammy on Lindsey's skin, and she wanted to grab Mary's hand and give it a squeeze or wrap her in a hug. She didn't. Instead, she just sat and waited.

"He pinned me to the floor," Mary said. "I was terrified. He told me that I'd been asking for it. That the way I walked around all flirty and smiley told him that I was just begging for it."

She blew out a breath. She shook her head. Her long reddish-brown curls danced around her shoulders, and she looked at Lindsey and gave her a wry smile.

"What he didn't realize was that I had a badass older brother in the navy who taught me how to defend myself. I kneed him in the junk, then I jammed my thumb in his eye until he screamed. We brawled until we were both bloody and sweaty, and I told him if he left, I wouldn't call the police."

One single tear slid out of Mary's eye, and Lindsey reached across and grabbed her hand. She squeezed her fingers and said, "Wow, you are my shero."

Mary busted out a laugh. "Thanks. I ended up quitting that job and moving all within a week's time. I couldn't make myself work with that guy, knowing that he knew where I lived. Yeah, I couldn't do it."

Lindsey nodded. She'd have done the same.

"I did go to my manager afterward," she said. "But he was friends with the creep, and he didn't believe me, so I didn't even bother going to the police. It was my word against his and back then, well, I knew how that was going to go."

"I'm so sorry, Mary," Lindsey said.

Mary shrugged. "It's not any different than most women's stories. I got lucky. I knew how to protect myself. And I made damn sure that every woman who worked at that bar knew exactly what he'd done. I didn't want him to do that to anyone else."

"You are so brave," Lindsey said.

"Maybe. The sad truth is that most women have to deal with this sort of thing at one time or another, and it's crap," Mary said. She patted Lindsey's hand with her free one. "The point I'm trying to make—and I do have one—is that you, like me, didn't do anything wrong. This guy has no right to follow you home or put you in a position where you have to reject his attention. It's total BS."

"Thank you, I needed to hear that," Lindsey said. She dropped Mary's hand and put her arm around her shoulders, giving her a firm squeeze. "Thank you for telling me your story. It never goes away, does it?"

"The fear? No, it doesn't," Mary said. "But don't you worry. We'll take care of this guy."

Josie gave a cry and threw her wooden block up into the air. It rolled on the grass, stopping a few feet away. She looked at them and clapped in delight.

"And by the time Josie grows up, maybe the world will have changed, and she won't have to deal with this stuff," Lindsey said.

"Exactly," Mary said. "At least, we can hope so."

"I noticed you and Mary had quite the deep conversation," Sully said. They were in the water taxi with Heathcliff, heading home. Lindsey was grateful her parents were staying with the Sullivans for a few days, as she didn't want to have to tell them about Aaron Grady.

"We did," she said. She raised her voice to be heard over the engine. Even though the sun had set, the air was still thick and hot. "I told her about the situation."

"Good," Sully said. "The more eyes on that guy, the better. I called the police station. Emma is out on rounds. Do you want to stop by tonight and leave a report with whoever is on duty or wait until morning to talk to her?"

"I already called her and left a message for her to stop by the library tomorrow," Lindsey said. When Sully opened his mouth to protest, she held up her hand and nodded. "She's patrolling tonight, and I don't think I need to pester her with this right this second. I'll fill her in tomorrow. I promise. I know it's important to start a file on the guy."

"It is," he said. "I know it may not feel like it, but it is."

As they approached the pier, Lindsey scanned the area, looking for Grady. She glanced at Sully and noted that he was doing the same thing. Thankfully, the dock was empty.

As Sully coasted the boat into a smooth landing, Heathcliff jumped for the dock, and Lindsey scrambled out after him to steady the boat. Sully tossed her the rope, and Lindsey began to tie up the bow while he hopped out and did the same with the stern. When the boat was secure, they crossed to the stairs that led up to the pier. Sully and Heathcliff took the lead, and Lindsey followed.

At the top, she glanced around again. The pier was empty except for the Blue Anchor, Mary and Ian's restaurant, at the end. The lights were on and the music was blaring. The sounds of conversation punctuated by the occasional laugh drifted out over the water at them.

"Looks like the coast is clear," Sully said. He

took Lindsey's hand in his, and they made their way down the pier to where he had parked his truck. Lindsey tried not to be jumpy, but when a door slammed nearby, she started. Sully glanced at her and she shrugged.

"Sorry," she said. "I'm just on edge, I guess."

He nodded. The look in his eyes was dead serious. "I suspect Mary told you about what happened to her."

Lindsey nodded. "It was awful, and I can't believe her manager didn't believe her and did nothing."

"Yeah, well, just because he didn't do anything doesn't mean nothing was done," Sully said.

Lindsey lifted her brows. They had reached the truck, and Sully opened her door and waited for her to climb in. When she was sitting on the seat, they were face-to-face.

"One of my old navy buddies had retired and was on the New Haven PD," he said. "He and I had a chat with that guy, and I'm sure he never pulled another stunt like that again."

"Because you beat him up?" Lindsey asked. Try as she might, she couldn't feel sorry for a man who had assaulted her friend.

"Well, that and my friend made sure that the guy was watched by every cop working in that area. If that guy so much as sneezed in the direction of a woman, he was seen."

Lindsey reached forward and hugged her man.

"Mary sure got lucky when she got you for a brother."

"We'll see if you still think that tomorrow," he said.

"Why? What's happening tomorrow?"

"You are going to start training in self-defense," he said.

"What?" Lindsey asked.

"Uh-huh," he said. "And not just you. Your entire library staff is going to learn some down-and-dirty self-defense tricks."

"We are?"

"Yup."

Lindsey met his gaze. Her usually mellow, laid-back future husband had his stubborn face on. It was a look she had seen very rarely, but the few times it had made its appearance, there'd been no talking him out of whatever he'd just made up his mind to do. She thought about her staff and realized that they were predominantly women, they worked nights, and they were frequently alone. She nodded.

"I think that's an excellent idea," she said.

Before the library opened the next morning, Lindsey held an impromptu staff meeting to inform them of the self-defense training that would be happening. She greeted Ms. Cole, Paula, Ann Marie, Beth and two of their part-time staff members when they came in the back door.

She had made a large pot of coffee and brought in muffins and fresh fruit from the bakery down the street.

Because the largest open space in the library was the story time room, they gathered there. To Lindsey's surprise, Robbie Vine joined Sully to teach the class. Robbie was a rather famous British actor who had come to Briar Creek several years before to raise his son.

Robbie had tried to get Lindsey to date him, but her heart had always belonged to Sully, and Robbie had found a fiery connection with Briar Creek's chief of police, Emma Plewicki. Over the past couple of years, Robbie had become one of Lindsey's closest friends. And while he and Sully liked to give each other a hard time, she had noticed over the past few months that the two men were becoming "mates," as Robbie would say. Sully had even included Robbie in his monthly fishing excursions with the guys.

While Sully explained that he and Robbie were going to share a few self-defense techniques, Lindsey met Robbie's gaze and lifted her eyebrows. He hit her with his patented star-power grin. He ran a hand through his strawberry blond hair, and his pale green eyes sparkled with mischief. Then he leaned close and said, "Sailor boy told me what's happening. If you need me to shadow you just give me a holler."

"Thanks," she said. "I'm planning to see Emma

71

today, and I'm hoping that she can check his behavior and it won't have to go any further than that."

"Stalkers," Robbie said. "I've had my share. They really don't get it until you get right in their face. It's unfortunate but true."

Lindsey sighed. She feared he was right.

"Robbie, over here," Sully said. He waved Robbie over to him, and Lindsey moved to join the rest of her staff members, who were sitting in chairs in a circle to watch the demonstration.

"Robbie and I are going to show you some quick getaway techniques if you find yourself alone with a patron who puts you in an untenable situation."

"More accurately, you mean if someone traps you in a corner and cops a feel?" Ms. Cole asked.

Everyone's head swiveled in her direction. She kept staring at Sully, who nodded. "Yes, good example."

Ms. Cole crossed her arms and looked at the rest of them. "I've been around a long time. I wish we'd had training like this twenty years ago. We used to have this one patron who would try to get you alone in the back of the stacks, and he'd grab your bum when you bent down to get a book for him off the bottom shelf. We complained but were told to take it as a compliment. I did not." She glowered. "One day I just snapped, and before he could grab me, I spun around with a book in hand and nailed him right in the privates. It was a very big book."

Both Sully and Robbie grimaced.

"Then I told him if he ever did that to anyone again, I was going to tell his wife."

Paula held up her fist, and Ms. Cole looked at her in confusion. Paula wagged her fist and said, "Knuckle bump, Ms. Cole."

"I think not," Ms. Cole said, and she reached over and somberly shook Paula's fist, causing Beth to burst out laughing, while Ann Marie snorted and Lindsey grinned. The other staff members, who were new and still in awe of Ms. Cole, looked nervous.

"I must say, well done, Ms. Cole," Robbie said. That was all he got out before Sully grabbed him from behind, pinning his arms to his sides.

"Ah!" Robbie shrieked.

"Try and break out," Sully said.

Robbie wriggled and wiggled. He tried to step on Sully's foot, but Sully evaded him. Lindsey watched the two men grapple and struggle. They were well matched in size and strength. Robbie broke one arm free and managed to hook it around Sully's head, bending them both over. Their faces were red, and sweat beaded up on their foreheads as they scuttled across the floor like a crab with a bad sense of direction.

"Is it wrong for me to picture them with their shirts off while they do this?" Ann Marie asked.

"Yes, you're objectifying our self-defense teachers," Paula said. But she was smiling.

"Quit moving, sailor boy," Robbie snapped when Sully slipped from his hold.

"You quit moving, you overgrown ham," Sully returned. "We're supposed to show them how to break a hold, not try to get their aggressor into a headlock."

"Argh."

"Humph."

The two men continued to tussle and grunt, much to the amusement of the assembled staff.

"Why are my boyfriend and your fiancé putting on the most boring mixed martial arts match ever?"

5

Lindsey turned her head to see the chief of police, Emma Plewicki, standing there. Emma had been dating Robbie for a while now, and it was clear from the look on her face that the man still charmed her silly even when he was being an idiot.

"It was supposed to be a demonstration on self-defense, but it turned into . . ." Lindsey gestured at the two men.

"What not to do," Emma said. "Got it."

She strode over to where Robbie and Sully were huffing and puffing while trying to—well, at this point, it was hard to figure out what they were trying to do.

Emma grabbed a hand—Lindsey wasn't sure whose—and said, "A quick release technique is to find the soft part of your captor's hand, the fleshy part between the thumb and index finger, and then dig into it." She demonstrated, and there was a yelp that seemed to come from Robbie. "Once they release you, go for their more vulnerable spots." She lifted her heavily booted foot and brought it down on an instep, which looked like Sully's. There was a grunt. "Then you can go for a finishing blow, and a solid punch or knee to the thigh will disable your assailant." Emma demonstrated, and Robbie dropped to the ground. "Of course, a thumb in the eye socket will render your attacker useless."

She reached toward Sully, who had the presence of mind to tuck and roll away from her. He popped up on his feet with his hands in the air.

"And that's a wrap, as my friend would say," Sully said. He reached down and pulled Robbie to his feet. Robbie's leg was still rubbery from Emma's charley horse, so Sully draped Robbie's arm over his shoulders and hauled him toward the door. He glanced at Lindsey and said, "Call you later."

Lindsey nodded, trying not to laugh as the two men hurried away as if afraid Emma was going to chase after them and do some more damage.

At the door, Robbie paused to glance at his girl and with a wink said, "I can't wait for round two, love."

Emma blushed a faint shade of pink and then shook her head at him. "Idiot."

Once the men were gone, she turned back to the room. "Fancy moves aside, if ever you find yourself in a vulnerable situation, the number-one thing you can do to help yourself is make noise. Make it as difficult as possible for your attacker, scream, kick, punch, fight. Most attackers are counting on your shock and surprise to keep you docile. They'll threaten you with 'Be quiet and I'll let you go.'" She shook her head. "If they've grabbed you, they aren't going to let you go. Fight like your life depends upon it, because it probably does. That being said, the odds of being attacked by a stranger are slim—about fifteen percent, according to the Bureau of Justice Statistics, so while it's good to be prepared, you don't have to make yourself crazy. Just be aware of your surroundings and act accordingly. The much more likely scenario is that a woman will be attacked or harmed by a man she knows, and that is much harder to guard against, because they aren't strangers."

There was a grim twist to Emma's lips, and Lindsey knew that as a police officer, she was in the thick of domestic situations all the time. It had to get old.

"The librarian in me appreciates your stats," Lindsey said.

"I thought you might," Emma said.

"We have fifteen minutes until opening," Ms. Cole said. She rose from her seat and gestured everyone toward the door. "Let's go."

They all rose and headed back to work.

"Lindsey, do you have a minute to talk now?" Emma asked.

"She does," Beth said. She gave Lindsey a look. "I'll oversee opening. You need to get Emma up to speed."

"Thanks, I'll be out as soon as I can," Lindsey said. She gestured for Emma to sit down.

The door shut behind her staff, and Lindsey took the chair beside Emma. She told her what had been happening with Aaron Grady, and Emma nodded, pursing her lips and raising her eyebrows at the weird text and the sight of Grady on the pier, watching Lindsey on Sully's boat.

"I feel like an idiot complaining about him, because he hasn't threatened me," Lindsey said. "But I just can't shake the feeling that his interest in me is not normal."

"The flowers, showing up at your house, sending the text message while you were shopping for your wedding dress—assuming it was him—all indicate a fixation that isn't welcome, whether there is a threat or not," Emma said. "You were very direct with him that you didn't appreciate his interest, so he backed off, but obviously, he isn't getting it. I'll have a talk with him and see if I can get a read on him and make it clear that he is to keep his distance."

Lindsey felt the tension inside of her uncoil. She wasn't overreacting. Emma was going to step in. She felt better for the first time in days.

"Thank you, I really appreciate that," she said.

"I want you to keep a log of everything he has said and done to make you uncomfortable," Emma said. "If he shows up at the library with more flowers, if you get any weird texts, if you see him watching you or think he's following you, write it down with the date and time," Emma said. "We want to have a concrete record of harassment."

"Is it harassment, or is he just socially defective?" Lindsey asked.

"Doesn't matter," Emma said. "If he's making you uncomfortable, then it has to stop."

Lindsey nodded. She'd definitely feel better if she wasn't looking over her shoulder all the time, waiting for Grady to spring out at her.

"All right," Lindsey said. "I'll make a list."

It didn't take very long to write down the dates and times of her interactions with Grady. In fact, when she was finished, she wondered whether she was overreacting. She felt somewhat stupid and silly, as if this was all a misunderstanding and she was being a drama queen, rejecting the offer of friendship from a person who was a little off.

But then she thought about the text message when she was getting her wedding dress. She hadn't recognized the number. She hadn't been able to trace the number on her own, and Emma hadn't gotten back to her about it either. She couldn't think of anyone else who would send her a message like that. It was creepy and weird, and her gut told her that it was from Grady.

Her morning was spent going over the schedule

for the rest of the summer. Because they were a small library with limited full-time employees, they took turns working on the evenings that the library was open. Since it was summer, Lindsey had to factor in vacations and extra days off to be certain they had a full-timer in the building all the nights they were open. Because she, Beth and Ms. Cole were the senior employees, it was up to them to cover the extra nights when they were short staffed.

She'd gotten through most of August's calendar by the time she had to start her shift at the reference desk. She gathered the stack of library periodicals she planned to read—she was looking for some ideas to spark more outreach in the community—and headed out the door to the desk. It was midday, and Ann Marie was due for her lunch break.

"I'm tagging in," she said as she approached Ann Marie and a library patron. Valerie Cannata, who was one of Lindsey's favorites, had recently taken up knitting. She mostly worked on scarves, which she called blankets for snakes, but she was looking to branch out into more challenging projects.

"I can finish," Ann Marie said.

"Nah, I've got this," Lindsey said. "Go have lunch."

"Yay, I'm starving," Ann Marie said. "I follow an author online, and she frequently posts about bad breakfast choices, and today she had cherry pie. Ever since then, the cheesecake in my lunch has been calling my name. To heck with the ham sandwich."

"Life is uncertain—eat dessert first," Valerie said.

"Agreed," Lindsey laughed.

She took over the search and handed Valerie a slip of paper with the pertinent call numbers for knitting. She then walked her into the shelves to show her exactly where the books were. Once Valerie was immersed in the section, Lindsey returned to the desk. She sat down and did a visual sweep of the library.

Ms. Cole was chatting with a patron at the checkout desk. Beth was wrangling kids in the children's area, the local genealogical society had filled up one of the study rooms, and Paula was changing the bulletin board in the lobby.

Notices for local yard sales, missing pets, neighborhood-watch meetings and so forth were posted every month, and Paula had taken it upon herself to be the liaison. It was a pretty straight-forward process—take down the old and put up the new—but occasionally, it got interesting, such as the time Mike Willoughby had tried to sell Trevor Kendall's lawn mower because he'd left it out in his front yard one too many times.

"Just ask her, Leigh."

"I can't, Sorayah. I'm too embarrassed."

Lindsey heard the whispered conversation behind her, but she didn't turn around. She could tell by the high pitched voices that they were teenagers, and she figured they were talking about her, but she didn't want to scare them off by appearing too eager to help. She waited until they got a little closer, and then she tried to engage them with her friendliest smile.

"Hi, can I help you?" she asked. She was right. They were teenagers. If she had to guess, she'd place them at about fifteen, maybe sixteen. They were both brunette and dressed in shorts and sleeveless blouses.

"No," one said at the same time the other said, "Yes."

They stared at each other, and Lindsey waited. Finally, the staring contest ended, and one of the girls asked, "How can you look up if a person is who they say they are on the internet?"

"You mean how do you verify their identity?" Lindsey asked.

"Yes," the other one said. "That."

"I suppose it depends upon what you know about them," Lindsey said. "If you know their name and address, there are a million different ways to search for them."

"Leigh only has his first name and his handle."

"Handle?"

"Yeah, you know, the handle he goes by on social media. He calls himself—"

"Sorayah, shh." Leigh glanced around the library. It was clear she didn't want anyone to overhear this conversation. Sorayah rolled her eyes. Lindsey tried not to smile.

"What do you know about him?" Lindsey asked.

"His name is Josh, but his handle is Pancake-Boy," Leigh whispered. "Oh, and I have his picture."

"And you want to know if he's legit?" Lindsey asked.

"He's been asking her out," Sorayah said. "But he is way too hot to be interested in a high school sophomore."

"Thanks a lot," Leigh said. She tossed her hair over her shoulder.

"I'm trying to be a good friend," Sorayah said. "I don't want to see you abducted by some psycho who preys on teen girls."

"But he writes the nicest things," Leigh said. "He says he loves my eyes and my smile."

"That is very sweet, but your friend is right," Lindsey said. "You can't be too careful online. Without more information, the easiest way to discover whether Josh is for real is to do a reverse image search."

"You can do that?" Leigh asked.

"Yeah, it's pretty simple," Lindsey said. She gestured for the two girls to look at her monitor. She opened up the free search for images, and then opened a second window. "Can you bring up his photo here? I'll need to upload it into the search engine."

"Yeah," Leigh said. She sounded reluctant, as if afraid that her dreams were about to be shattered.

Lindsey moved aside so the teen could find his picture. When the girl brought up the photo, Lindsey had to school her features to keep from showing any emotion. But, dang, this was not the photo of a typical teen boy. Oh, he was definitely a teenager, but the picture looked like a professional model with tousled hair, chiseled features, and smoldering eyes. Lindsey had a feeling Sorayah was right. This guy was not what he seemed.

From there it was a simple upload the image and click search. The browser did the hard work. In mere seconds, several matching pictures popped up. Lindsey clicked on the first one. It linked to a webpage that listed the boy in the picture as an Australian model. In fact, the picture "Josh" had used came right from an Australian magazine called *Frankie*. The model's name was Bruce, not Josh, and he was nineteen and lived in Sydney.

"I'm sorry, but it looks like Josh is not who he says he is," she said.

"I knew it," Sorayah said. "Probably, the person chatting with you is some pervy old man who is just waiting to ask you for nude selfies."

Leigh looked as if she might be ill. "I should have known. Why would any guy who looked like that be interested in me?"

"Hey," Lindsey said. "Don't think like that. I'm sure there are plenty of boys at school who would like you if you paid more attention to them instead of some stranger on the internet."

"Julian likes you," Sorayah said. "He asked you to prom and was nice even when you said no."

"I'm an idiot," Leigh said. She looked stricken. "I was so sure Josh was the one. I said no to Julian. So stupid!"

"Believing in love doesn't make you stupid," Lindsey said. "It makes you an optimist. There's nothing wrong with that, but it's probably more likely to be real when it's with a real person and not through a phone app, don't you think?"

Leigh nodded and Sorayah smiled. She threw her arm around her friend and said, "Come on—we must strategize your next play to get Julian to ask you out again."

"You're right," Leigh said. She glanced at the computer and studied the male model's photo. "I'm sorry, Josh, but I'm just not that into you anymore." She pulled out her phone and brought up "Josh's" profile, then she deleted him. She glanced at her friend and said, "Onward."

"Thank you, Ms. Librarian," Sorayah said.

"You can call me Lindsey."

"Thank you, Lindsey," Leigh said. She put her

hand over her heart. "Truly, that could have been a catastrophe."

"My pleasure," Lindsey said. She watched the two girls walk away with their heads pressed together as they plotted their next move. Not for the first time, she was so happy she wasn't single anymore. It was just too much work.

Lindsey opened her *Library Journal* and began to peruse the articles. She was halfway through a piece about community engagement when she had the peculiar sensation that someone was watching her. Dread thrummed through her. She didn't look up. She didn't want to know. She hoped desperately that she was wrong. She flipped the page in the magazine without reading the words.

As she did, she lifted her head. Her gaze was caught by a man sitting at the table ten feet from her desk. He was holding a gardening magazine and looking over the top of it—at her. Lindsey didn't have to do a double take to recognize Grady. He lowered the magazine and gave her a closed-lip smile. He looked perfectly normal, but Lindsey still felt a shiver ripple up her spine.

She pulled out the list she'd kept of his weird behavior and added the date and time and the fact that he was just sitting there, staring at her. She thought about calling Emma, but was staring at someone a criminal offense? He hadn't said anything or approached her, but he also wasn't reading. He was staring. At her. She ignored him completely. It went on for an hour.

When Ann Marie came back, Lindsey all but bolted from the service desk, seeking refuge in her office. She didn't know why Grady was able to rattle her like this, but she felt uncomfortable in her own skin. She dropped her periodicals onto her desk and let out a pent-up breath. Surely, Grady didn't think his behavior was okay. Should she have confronted him? She was going to have to. This was completely unacceptable.

She sank into her office chair and glanced out her office window. Lindsey's office had two large windows; one looked out over the workroom, and the other, the library. As she glanced at the book stacks, she saw Grady hauling a small table and a chair into the shelves. He turned them so that they faced her office, then he proceeded to sit and stare *into her office.*

When she met his gaze, he gave her the same closed-lip smile, and she had the feeling there was some whole other scenario going on in his head, but she had no idea what it was. She didn't know whether he meant her harm, whether he was just trying to harass her or whether he was completely unhinged behind his genial facade. It was unnerving with a pinch of terrifying.

Lindsey picked up the phone and called Emma. She'd had enough. She wasn't going to be nice anymore. When she explained what was happening, Emma interrupted.

"I'll be right there," she said.

Lindsey put down the phone, wondering whether she'd done the right thing. The introvert inside of her didn't want to cause a scene. Then she caught a glimpse of Grady, who was still staring, and she knew that she'd been right to call Emma. Clearly, he needed a voice of authority louder than hers telling him to keep his distance, because he wasn't listening.

Emma was there within minutes, and Lindsey wondered whether she'd been waiting for a call. From her office, Lindsey saw Emma approach Grady. She sat on the corner of his desk and leaned in. She had the pose of someone who was relaxed, but as they spoke, Lindsey could see Grady get a mutinous look on his face. Emma shook her head. She gestured to the door, and Grady glowered at her.

Lindsey glanced back down at her desk. She was feeling more and more on edge. Maybe she should have let it go. Maybe Grady would have gotten tired of watching her and just gone away. Then she thought about the text she'd received while shopping for her wedding dress. He wasn't going to just go away.

She reminded herself that she hadn't done anything to cause this and whatever happened was because Grady wasn't respecting the boundaries she'd set in place. What he was doing right now was straight-up creepy, and it had to be stopped. Feeling better, Lindsey tried to ignore what looked to be a heated exchange between Emma and Grady.

Out of the corner of her eye, she saw Emma stand with her arms crossed over her chest. Grady pushed back from the desk and stood, too. Then, with one last glare at Emma, he stalked away toward the front of the library. Emma followed him, and Lindsey folded her arms on her desk and put her head down with a sigh. Good. She hoped this would be the end of it.

It wasn't.

Lindsey was going over the agenda of the next library board meeting with the president, Milton Duffy, in the main part of the library when Mayor Hensen and his right-hand man, Herb Gunderson, came into the building. The mayor was known for his politician's thousand-watt smile, but at the moment, there was no sign of it. Not even a twitch of his lips.

"Good afternoon, Mayor, Herb," Lindsey greeted them.

"A word, Lindsey," Mayor Hensen said. He kept walking, not even slowing down, toward Lindsey's office. She gave Milton a wide-eyed look and followed the mayor into the back of the workroom, where her office was. She felt Ms.

Cole watching, and she turned and shrugged with a wide-eyed expression. Ms. Cole, who was not a fan of the mayor, smiled.

Once in the office, the mayor and Herb took the two seats across from her desk, and Lindsey sat down behind it.

"Can I get you anything?" she offered. "Coffee, water, soda?"

"No thank you," Mayor Hensen said. Herb didn't say anything, and Lindsey knew that the nature of their relationship meant that the mayor was answering for Herb as well.

"We're here to discuss a matter of concern brought to us by a resident of Briar Creek," Herb said.

Lindsey felt her heart sink. This was how they always began a discussion when someone wanted to ban a book. While the mayor and Herb tended to be more interested in placating the patron, Lindsey took a hard line on not banning books. Period.

She straightened her back. If they tried to get rid of one of her paperbound babies, well, there was going to be a fight.

"Mr. Aaron Grady stopped by my office and told us that he'd been banned from using the library by the chief of police," Mayor Hensen said. "Is this true?"

Lindsey felt her face get warm. She did not want to have to explain this situation to the mayor. It was awkward and embarrassing, and in a town where most of the department heads were male, she was afraid this was going to make her look weak and ineffectual. Her resentment spiked. She decided to stick to the facts.

"I believe Chief Plewicki spoke to him about his inappropriate behavior," Lindsey said. "Last I saw, she followed him out of the building, and I haven't heard from her since. I expect she'll be in touch to give me more details when she gets the chance. If she banned him from the building, that's welcome news to me."

"What was inappropriate about his use of the library?" Herb asked.

"At the time, he was sitting at a desk and staring at me," she said.

The two men exchanged a look.

"For an hour," Lindsey said. "Just staring. And when I came into my office after being out there, he dragged a desk and chair into the shelving so he could continue to do so."

She pointed out the window at the stacks, but the desk and chair had already been moved back to their original location.

"Do you think you might be overreacting?" Herb asked. Lindsey glowered.

"He brings me roses from his garden," she said. They stared at her, clearly waiting for more. "He pops up in town, wherever I am." They weren't getting it. "He showed up at my house."

The men exchanged a look. Herb cleared his throat and said, "Lindsey, you're an attractive woman, and I mean that as an unbiased observation of fact and not in any way inappropriately."

"Okay," Lindsey said. She wasn't sure what to make of this.

"So is it really unreasonable for a man to notice you?" Herb asked.

The mayor nodded as if to say, *What he said.*

"I mean," Herb continued, "can't you just take it as a compliment and not have him kicked out of the building?"

Lindsey returned their gazes, studying the two men sitting in front of her. She liked them. They were both good, solid family men. The sort who went to church every Sunday, doted on their moms, coached Little League and soccer in their spare time. They were solid, salt-of-the-earth types of guys. They could never imagine what it felt like to be a victim of unwanted attention, and Lindsey didn't know how to explain it beyond the truth that it sucked. She went with the facts.

"No, I can't," she said. "Because it's not a compliment. It's creepy and marginally threatening, and if it was your wife, sister, mother or daughter, I don't think you'd want them to put up with it either."

"Oh, now, come on," Mayor Hensen tried to cajole her. "I know I'd be delighted if a woman thought I was attractive enough to warrant a couple of longing looks and some roses. Surely, being complimented like that can't be that bad." He elbowed Herb. "Am I right?"

"Absolutely," Herb said. "We don't want to punish a man for having a silly little crush, do we? You should be flattered, Lindsey."

"Flattered?" she asked. "Did you miss the part where the guy showed up at my house with flowers when I was home alone? I never gave him my address. I'm not even listed at that address. That's crossing the line."

"Yes, he did admit that he might have over-stepped," Herb said.

"Might have?" Lindsey asked. "There's no 'might have' here. Listen, there's something wrong with him, and I'm not willing to put my staff or myself in harm's way if this guy decides to show up with a gun or a bomb or whatever. So no, I'm not going to pretend that I find this flattering. I don't. It's wrong and it's weird, and I expect your support on this."

The two men exchanged another look.

"Here's the problem," Herb said. "Mr. Grady has threatened to sue the town for infringing upon his civil rights if he is kicked out of the library. Since he hasn't threatened you in any way, we feel it is best to let him back into the building."

"You're joking," Lindsey said.

The two men simply looked at her, and she knew that their fear of a lawsuit outweighed their concern that she and her staff could be at risk. In that moment, the disappointment she felt in these two men she considered colleagues and friends had no bottom.

"I'm afraid not," Mayor Hensen said. "Mr. Grady is allowed to use the library, just like any other resident of Briar Creek and the Thumb Islands. I'll be making my position on this clear to Chief Plewicki as well."

He rose from his seat and Herb followed. At the door, Herb looked back and said, "If you have any other information, if he does anything that warrants further consideration, let us know, and we can discuss it again."

With that, they left, and Lindsey felt betrayed on a level she had never before experienced.

6

"I don't understand how they can care more about his right to use the library than your right to safety," Sully said. They were driving to the Blue Anchor since neither of them felt like cooking. "I'm going to have a talk with Mayor Hensen."

"I appreciate that," Lindsey said. "But I don't think it will do any good, and I feel as if I've already been labeled the problem child, and if my fiancé goes in to stick up for me, it only looks worse. So I'd rather you didn't."

Sully looked as if he was going to argue, but then he nodded. "I understand, but I really don't like this."

"I know you don't," she said. "Me either. I hate looking over my shoulder, wondering if he's there, just lurking."

He pulled into the lot and parked his truck under a streetlight. He came around the front of the truck and opened Lindsey's door for her. His face was creased with concern when he took her hand to help her step down.

"At the risk of sounding bossy," he said, "I'd prefer it if you didn't travel anywhere alone for a while. Since I'll be taking you to and from work, that's covered, but if I'm out on the water during the day, I want you to have backup. I talked to Robbie and he's at your disposal during the day."

"Thank you," she said. She would have said it wasn't necessary, but the fact that Grady had threatened to sue the town over his right to sit and stare at her made her think it was a good idea to use the buddy system for now.

Sully kept her hand in his as they strode into the restaurant. Ian Murphy waved to them from behind the bar as they entered, and Lindsey knew he'd send their usual drinks over as soon as they sat down. Fortunately, a small table by the window was available, and they were able to sit and enjoy the view of the bay and the islands as the evening sun set.

In an obvious effort to lift her spirits, Sully told her about the tour group he'd taken out that afternoon, complete with a funny story about one of his passengers, who suffered from a fear of deep, dark water, so much so that he refused to move from the center of the boat and had no interest in looking at anything on the tour. She felt her tension fall away.

"Why was he on the boat, then?" Lindsey asked.

"His wife insisted that he go because she wanted to do it," he said. "I genuinely felt bad for the guy. His fear was legit—pasty face, sweating profusely, the whole package."

"Why would his wife do that to him?" she asked.

"No idea, but my guess is that she didn't take his fear seriously," he said. "I promise I'll never do that to you after we're married—or ever, for that matter."

"Me, too," she said. "That's just cruel."

"I have a feeling they've been married for so long she's stopped thinking of him as his own person, and now he's just an extension of her, which was probably why she couldn't understand a fear she doesn't have herself," he said.

"You'd think it would be the other way," she said. "That she would understand him better since they've been married so long and that she would protect him from the things he fears."

"I know," he agreed. "They were definitely the oddest couple I have ever met."

Their first course arrived, and Lindsey felt her mouth water. The Blue Anchor was known for its fresh seafood, and tonight was no exception. Ian had hooked them up with crab cakes that were loaded with fresh crabmeat, a broth-based chowder with just a hint of cream in it, and a pan-seared cod filet with homegrown steamed asparagus. Divine.

It was while chomping down on a bite of asparagus that Lindsey felt what was beginning to be an old familiar creepy feeling. Someone was watching her. She knew it. She could feel it in the prickle at the back of her neck and the way her heart sped up like an early warning system. She didn't want to alarm Sully, so she said nothing. Maybe it was just her imagination. Perhaps it was another patron staring at her because she was out of the library. Sometimes this threw people off, to see her out in public, as if librarians were expected to live in the library.

She swallowed her asparagus. It went down hard. She picked up her glass of wine and took a sip, trying to ease the tightness in her throat. Then she lifted her napkin and dabbed her mouth, using the opportunity to look down and to her right and then down and to her left. Her gaze was immediately caught by a man sitting at the bar. Aaron Grady. His stool was swiveled away from the bar to face her. Again, he gave her a skeevy smile and then lifted his own glass of wine to her in a silent toast.

She broke eye contact immediately. She didn't know what to do. Should she confront him? Ignore him? Call him out for going to the mayor? She closed her eyes. She hated this. She hated being made to feel vulnerable.

"Are you all right?" Sully asked. "You look pale. Do you want me to take you home?"

Lindsey opened her eyes. The concern in Sully's gaze was a balm. Just his being here made her feel better. Surely, Grady would be able to see that Lindsey had a wonderful, loving man in her life and that whatever it was Grady wanted from her was not going to happen—ever.

She supposed she could pretend that nothing was wrong and not tell Sully that Grady was here, but then she was lying to her fiancé for a man who was doing his level best to haunt her every waking hour. She wasn't going to do that.

"Grady's here," she said. "Sitting at the bar."

Sully's head whipped in that direction. "I can assume he's the one in the pressed shirt and pants who is staring at you?"

"Yup."

Sully snatched his napkin out of his lap and pushed back his chair in one motion. "I think it's time I had a chat with him."

"Are you sure that's a good idea?" she asked. "He's already threatening to sue the town—"

"I'm not the town," Sully said. "Sit tight. I'll be right back."

"Oh, no, I need for him to know that I am with you one hundred percent. I don't want him to skew it in his mind that you were confronting him on your own. I want him to know you have my full support," she said. She pushed back her chair and stood, too.

"Fair enough," Sully said.

Together they crossed the restaurant. Sully looked deceptively calm, but the muscle ticking in his clenched jaw let Lindsey know he was trying to keep his frustration with the situation in check.

"Aaron Grady?" he asked him as he stopped in front of him.

Grady kept his gaze on Lindsey, not even acknowledging Sully.

"Hi, Lindsey, you look lovely tonight," Grady said. He stared at her as if she were there to meet him and he was delighted.

She shook her head. "Mr. Grady, I've been very clear that your constant presence and staring makes me uncomfortable. I am asking you to respect my wishes and stop."

"Stop? But why?" Grady asked. He blinked at her, clearly confused.

Sully stepped in front of Lindsey and loomed over the smaller man. "She just told you that you are making her uncomfortable. You need to stop following her and stop staring at her. This isn't a suggestion. If I see you anywhere near her again, I'll feel compelled to make my point more decisively."

"Are you threatening me?" Grady asked. "Who do you think you are?"

"I'm the man who is going to marry her," Sully said.

Grady gave him a supercilious smile. "Maybe."

Sully glowered. "There's no 'maybe' about it. And let me be clear: I'm not threatening you. I promise you, if you come near her again, I will do whatever it takes to keep you away."

Grady ignored him, looking past him at Lindsey. "You can do much better than this."

Sully took a half step forward, raising his fist as he did so. Lindsey heard a gasp from a woman nearby, and she grabbed Sully's arm and held him back. She was not about to let him get arrested over this, as nice as it would have been to have him punch some sense or fear into Grady.

"Problem here?" Ian asked from behind the bar.

"This is Aaron Grady, the guy who's been harassing Lindsey," Sully said.

Ian snapped his bar rag off his shoulder and dropped it onto the bar. Several customers turned to watch the altercation.

"Right." He took the half-finished glass of wine from in front of Grady and poured it down the drain behind the bar. "That's it, then. I'll ask you to leave once, Mr. Grady, and if you refuse, I'll assist you out," Ian said. It was obvious from his tone that *assist* was a euphemism for *toss*.

"You can't do that," Grady protested. "I'll have your job. Where's the manager?"

"You're looking at him," Ian said. "I'm also the owner, so let me clarify that you aren't welcome in here any longer. Now go."

Grady scowled. He slid off his barstool and stiffly turned away from Ian. His gaze lingered on Lindsey. Then he gave her his usual smarmy smile and said, "I'll see you tomorrow, Lindsey."

No one moved until the door shut behind him. Sully turned and tucked Lindsey into his side. "Are you okay?"

"I'm fine," she said. "Creeped out but fine."

"What is that guy's deal?" Ian asked.

"I don't know, but he's going to stop harassing Lindsey," Sully said. "I plan to make sure of it."

Several customers were eavesdropping, and Lindsey felt the need to get everyone's attention off her. "We'll see Chief Plewicki tomorrow. I'm sure she can take care of the situation." Then she forced a smile and dragged Sully back to their table. She wanted nothing more than to put the whole thing behind them.

Despite the dessert that Ian sent over to their table, there was no saving their dinner. Lindsey felt jittery, and even though Sully tried to rally, she could tell he was still furious with Grady for his behavior toward Lindsey.

They finished the strawberry shortcake and didn't linger over coffee. Lindsey knew they were both eager to get home, away from the furtive glances of their fellow diners and the possibility that Grady would pop up again.

Sully paid their tab, and they headed to the door with a wave at Ian. Lindsey went to push through the door, but it was yanked open before she got there. A woman strode into the restaurant.

She was middle-aged, with stylishly cut gray hair and glasses. She wore a collared blouse in a pretty shade of pale green with khaki capris and sandals. Lindsey moved aside to let her pass, but the woman looked her up and down and then curled her lip in a faint sneer.

"You're her, aren't you?" she asked.

"Excuse me?" Lindsey said.

"You're the woman who is trying to steal my man," the woman spat. "I'm Sylvia Grady, Aaron's wife, and I know all about you, Lindsey Norris. You're a husband stealer."

Lindsey felt her face get hot in embarrassment as everyone in the restaurant turned to stare. Then her temper kicked in. She was about as far from a husband stealer as a nun was, and she refused to let this woman humiliate her.

"I'm sorry, but you're mistaken," she said. She was pleased that her voice came out calm and controlled. "I'm about to get married, and I can assure you, I have no interest in anyone but my fiancé."

"Pfft." Sylvia puffed out a breath through her teeth, dismissing Lindsey's words. It was too much.

"Don't," Lindsey snapped. She was furious. "I can't imagine why you would ever think that I could have any interest in your husband when I am marrying this man." She reached behind her and grabbed Sully's hand in hers, pulling him forward. "Honestly, why would I ever look at another guy when I have him? He's smart, funny, kind, well-read and the handsomest man I have ever known, so please save your 'pfft.' I promise you, Sully is the only man for me."

Sylvia glanced at Sully. She opened her mouth and then closed her mouth. Her lips compressed into a thin, tight line, then she tipped her chin up and stared at Lindsey in defiance. "Well, you're obviously one of those women who gets off on wrecking other people's marriages. You should be ashamed of yourself." Then she looked at Sully. "And you should find yourself a better woman than this one."

Lindsey reared back as if the woman had slapped her. Then she felt her own hand clench into a fist. She'd never hit another person in her life, but she was seriously tempted. Luckily, Sully was there to hold her back just like she had done for him.

"Mrs. Grady, let me be clear: there is no better woman for me than Lindsey, and I won't listen to you slam her with lies. As for your husband, nothing could be further from the truth," Sully said. "He is the one who is out of order. Lindsey has made it very clear to him that she is uncom-fortable with his attention. I suggest you save your anger for him, not my fiancée."

"You poor, foolish man," Sylvia said. She made a *tut-tut* noise, as if Sully was just some poor slob destined to be cheated on. "You're doomed for heartbreak. Mark my words—she'll ruin you." Then she turned toward Lindsey. "Stay away from my husband."

Before Lindsey could respond, Sylvia turned and slammed back out the front door. Lindsey knew without turning around that everyone was staring at her. She refused to acknowledge it. Instead, she squeezed Sully's hand in hers and said, "Are you ready? Because I am desperate to get home."

"Roger that," Sully said. He pushed the door open, and they left without looking back.

Sully was up and gone before Lindsey rose the next morning at six thirty. She found a cup of coffee and a note on the nightstand.

Today will be better, I promise. Also, Robbie is coming to take you to work. Call me if you need me. Be careful.
  Love you, Sully

Better? Lindsey figured it couldn't get much worse. After their altercations with both Gradys, Lindsey had been left feeling frustrated and vulnerable. She resented Sylvia Grady's insinuation and was angry that Aaron Grady had put her in this position. She had done nothing but her job, and here she was being stalked, accused and left feeling victimized. This was simply not okay.

She dressed carefully in her best business attire. She was going to the mayor's office today, and she was going to demand that he ban Aaron Grady from the library. She didn't care if the guy sued. She'd take her chances in front of a judge. There was simply no way she could work under the present conditions, and if she had to leave her job, so be it. Knowing this was a distinct possibility made her heartsick, but Lindsey knew that she couldn't go on like this. So there it was. She was going to have to force the mayor to choose between her and Grady. She dreaded finding out who he'd choose.

Robbie knocked on her door promptly at seven thirty. He was standing there, holding a coffee and a muffin, and he didn't even drop them when Heathcliff launched himself at him for his usual exuberant greeting.

Lindsey took the coffee and the muffin so Robbie could use both hands to pet Heathcliff. Her puppy accepted nothing less as he hugged Robbie around the knee with his paws and barked all his latest news at Robbie.

"Is that so, boy?" Robbie asked. Heathcliff licked him. "Tell me more."

Heathcliff barked and wagged and then wriggled loose to run around the front yard a few times. When he lapped back, he resumed hugging Robbie's knee and barked a few more times until

Robbie pulled a dog biscuit out of his pocket and handed it to the puppy, who charged inside and flopped onto his dog bed to enjoy his cookie in peace.

"You spoil him," Lindsey said.

"Sure," he said. "I'm not the one who buys him his own ice cream or had Nancy knit him a sweater."

"He gets cold in the winter," Lindsey said. "And the ice cream is Sully, not me."

"Uh-huh," Robbie said. "You're both pitiful over that mutt."

"Takes one to know one." Lindsey laughed. She turned and locked up the house, telling Heathcliff to be good. "Hey, thanks for giving me a lift today."

"My pleasure," he said. "Emma and I talked about your admirer, and we're both concerned. You're going to have to be very careful until he gets the message."

"I know," Lindsey sighed. "I just thought if I was direct, he would catch on."

Robbie held open the passenger-side door, and Lindsey climbed in. She took a sip of her coffee—perfection—while he walked around and slid into the driver's seat.

"Here's the thing, pet," Robbie said. "From my own experience, I've learned that the person with the fixation isn't operating in reality. They think they have a relationship with you when in truth they don't even know you. They've created some sort of alternate reality in their own mind, and nothing you say will dissuade them."

"Exactly," Lindsey said. "I keep trying to figure out what I did to cause this, but I only did a reference search for information on roses. That's it."

Robbie navigated the roads through town with ease. The traffic was minimal, as school was out and the summer tourists were still asleep.

"For the more rabid types, the only thing that works is to shut them down. Once they start crossing the line, you have to hold firm and refuse to engage with them in any way."

"Weren't you kidnapped by an overzealous fan once?" Lindsey asked.

"Yeah, that was mental," he said. "But not nearly as bad as the woman who showed up at my house with a gun. She was convinced I was a fake Robbie Vine who had murdered the real Robbie Vine, and she was going to kill me. Crazy."

"I'm not sure if this is making me feel better or worse," she said.

"Don't worry," Robbie said as he pulled into the parking lot. "We have a whole schedule set up between me, sailor boy, Ian and Charlie, to keep an eye on you until the nutjob goes away."

"I hate that this is causing everyone grief," she said.

"No worries. This is what friends do for each other." He parked the car and patted her shoulder. "Come on—I'm on duty all morning until Ian tags in at noon."

Lindsey clutched her coffee, her muffin and her purse as she stepped out of the car. She took one step toward the building and froze. Sitting outside the back door, propped up against the wall, waiting for her, was Aaron Grady. Robbie glanced from her to Grady and swore.

"Get back in the car and call Emma," he said. "I'll go chat with him."

"I don't think that's a good idea," she said. "What if he's armed?"

"I'll charm him," Robbie said, looking anything but charming. "Do it."

Lindsey reluctantly climbed back into the car. She put down her coffee and muffin and fumbled for her phone, glancing at Robbie as she did. He approached Grady with his hands out in a placating gesture. Grady didn't move, didn't acknowledge him in any way. A shiver went down her spine. She found Emma's phone number and pressed "Call."

She held the phone up to her ear as she watched Robbie bend down as if offering to help Grady up. Except he didn't. Instead, Robbie jumped back. He turned and ran toward her.

"Lindsey, what's up?" Emma answered the call.

"Hang on," Lindsey said. She pushed open the door and stood. "Robbie, what is it?"

"Grady," Robbie said. He was short of breath, and his words came out on an exhale. "He's dead."

7

What?" Emma cried. "Where are you?"

"The library."

"I'll be right there," Emma said. "Put Robbie on."

Lindsey handed over the phone. She sank back into the passenger seat, feeling the shock roll over her. Grady was dead. At the back entrance to her library.

"We thought he was sitting and waiting for Lindsey," Robbie explained the situation to Emma. "So I went to chat with him, but he didn't respond. When I got close enough, I could see he'd been shot in the chest, but there's no weapon near him that I could see. Whoever did it took the time to pose him so that he's sitting as if waiting for Lindsey. Grisly stuff."

He glanced at Lindsey while he spoke. His eyes were kind but also worried, as if he couldn't wrap his head around what was happening. Well, that made two of them. Who would have shot Grady? And why at the back of the library? Had he shot himself? Was that even possible? Lindsey felt her stomach roll, and she feared she was going to be sick. Her staff would be arriving in a few minutes. What was she going to say?

The sound of sirens grew louder, and a police car whipped into the parking lot, followed by another cruiser and an ambulance. The EMTs hopped out and began to grab their equipment. Emma, still on the phone with Robbie, dashed past them to the body.

"I'll be right back," Emma called. She tucked her phone into her pocket, and Robbie handed Lindsey's back to her.

Robbie and Lindsey watched as the paramedics and the officers swarmed Grady. Officer Kirkland, who'd been in the second car, began to cordon off the area with yellow crime scene tape. The EMTs left, realizing there was very little they could do and that this was now a job for the medical examiner.

A second wave of nausea forced Lindsey to put her head between her knees. She was wearing a tailored skirt, so this wasn't as easy as it could have been. She began to sweat in the hot, humid air, and she took off her jacket and put it on the seat behind her. She wanted to call Sully, but he was out on his tour boat and wouldn't be back for hours. She didn't want him to fret while he was out there.

"It's going to be all right," Robbie said. "Emma is brilliant. She'll figure this all out."

"I hope so," she said.

"Wait here," he said. "I'll go see what she can tell us."

Lindsey nodded. She didn't know how to feel about Grady being shot and killed. It was horrible, no doubt. But she *did* know that she wasn't going to have to look over her shoulder anymore, and she wasn't sorry about that.

Unfortunately, unless Grady had committed suicide, there were going to be a lot of questions. Number one being who had murdered him. The showdown between Sully and Grady at the Blue Anchor last night had been witnessed by most of the town. Had they heard Sully threaten Grady? She knew that it had been a hollow threat—Sully would never have hurt Grady—but would the rest of the town stand by Sully? She didn't know.

She saw Ms. Cole and Beth arrive in the parking lot at the same time. Beth, like Lindsey, had always ridden a bike to work, and she did today, too, despite the heat. She rode her cruiser right up to Lindsey. She stopped and lowered her sunglasses. She glanced from the crime scene tape to Lindsey and back.

"What's going on?" she asked.

There were so many people in the area that Grady's body was no longer visible. Lindsey glanced past Beth and saw Ms. Cole coming their way. She was dressed in her usual monochromatic fashion, as if everything matched when it was technically the same color. Today's color was teal or aqua; Lindsey wasn't sure, because Ms. Cole had both happening, from her teal shoes to her aqua skirt to her teal and white striped blouse.

Beth glanced over her shoulder and saw Ms. Cole and then turned back to Lindsey. It was clear she understood that Lindsey was waiting for Ms. Cole to join them before explaining.

"Just tell me this," Beth said. "Are you okay?"

"Yeah." Lindsey nodded. "I'm all right." It felt like a fib, a big one, but she hoped that if she said it often enough, it would become true.

"Good morning," Ms. Cole said. She glanced from Lindsey to the building and back.

"We have a situation," Lindsey said. "When Robbie and I arrived this morning, we found Aaron Grady sitting outside the back door of the library."

"Oh no," Beth said. Her eyes were huge. "He didn't harm you, did he?"

"No," Lindsey said. "Robbie went to talk to him while I called Emma. I thought she should be involved."

"Very wise," Ms. Cole said. "His behavior definitely warrants some police interference."

"Yes, well, when Robbie approached him, he discovered that he'd been shot and killed," Lindsey said. "The police are investigating now."

Beth gasped, and Ms. Cole's eyebrows shot up on her forehead.

"But who? Wait . . . here? He was shot *here?*" Beth cried.

"No, he wasn't," Emma said. She stepped into their group, with Robbie beside her. "The crime scene techs are certain he was shot somewhere else and delivered here, trying to make it look like his murder was tied to Lindsey, no doubt."

"You mean, they tried to make it look like *I* killed him?" Lindsey asked.

"I'm guessing you or someone close to you," Emma said.

"Sully." Lindsey met the chief of police's gaze and didn't look away.

"Perhaps," Emma said. She turned to Beth and Ms. Cole. "There is no indication that anything happened inside of the library. You're free to open the building as usual today, but don't come through the back door until the crime scene personnel are done. I'll let you know when that is."

Both women looked to Lindsey. She tried to sound calm as if it were business as usual as she said, "Go ahead and open up. I'll be there as soon as I can."

Beth gave her a considering look, but Lindsey forced a small smile, hoping she looked reassuring and not as if she was unraveling. It must have worked, because Ms. Cole gave a brisk nod and turned on her heel, heading for the front door with Beth hurrying behind her.

"Lindsey, I have some questions for you," Emma said. She sounded regretful, as if she hated to ask but had no choice. "Where were you this morning?"

"At home until Robbie picked me up," she said. "I woke up at six thirty. Sully was already gone since he had an early-morning boat tour around the islands."

"Did you see Sully this morning?" Emma asked.

"No, but he left me a cup of coffee and a note," she said. "I know what you're thinking, and I know you know that it isn't true."

Emma tipped her head to the side. "What am I thinking?"

"That Sully had something to do with this, but he didn't."

"Why would I think that?" Emma's tone was infuriating, and Lindsey lost her temper.

"Don't do that," she snapped. "Don't go all chief of police on me. You know me, you know Sully, and you know we had nothing to do with this."

"Easy now, ladies, there's no need to throw a wobbler," Robbie said. His British accent was turned up to extra-soothing. It didn't work.

"Hush," Emma hissed at him at the same time Lindsey said, "Shh."

Robbie threw his hands in the air as if exasperated.

"I know you didn't have anything to do with this," Emma said. "And I know Sully didn't either, but I am the chief of police, and just because I believe you doesn't mean I can treat you any differently than I would any other person of interest. And because of Grady's obsession with you, like it or not, both you and Sully are persons of interest. So we will do this by the book so that there is no doubt that the investigation has been handled without bias. Am I clear?"

"I'm sorry," Lindsey said. "Of course, you're right."

"So do you have any knowledge of Sully's whereabouts this morning before you woke up?" Emma asked.

"No, I don't," Lindsey said. For just a second she debated lying and saying that she saw Sully off that morning. It was a stupid idea, because she was a terrible liar, but also, the truth always came out. She knew that. Even worse, she knew it would be a wasted effort because when Emma questioned Sully, she knew without a doubt, he would tell the whole truth and nothing but the truth because that was the sort of man he was. She was just going to have to trust Emma and the system whether she liked it or not.

"Come on," Robbie said. "Let's go inside and have a cup of tea. It'll calm your nerves."

Emma and Lindsey exchanged a glance.

"It won't," Emma said. "But it'll give you

117

something to do. I'll stop in when we're done here."

"Hey, Chief Plewicki!" Officer Kirkland shouted to her from the side of the building. He was bent over a thick patch of azalea bushes. He popped up and waved her over.

"Excuse me," Emma said. She jogged over to Kirkland.

Not to be left out of what was happening around her library, Lindsey followed with Robbie trailing after her. Kirkland was wearing blue latex gloves, and dangling from his loose grip was a handgun.

"I think we have our murder weapon," Kirkland said.

"Oh my God, they just threw it in the bushes?" Lindsey gasped. "What if a child had found it?"

"Bag it," Emma said. "We'll need the ballistics to verify that it matches the bullets that killed Grady."

Kirkland nodded and dropped the gun into an evidence bag before taking it to the crime scene techs.

"You need to leave," Emma said to Lindsey. "I can't have the crime scene compromised by your presence."

Her tone was harsh, and Lindsey sent Robbie a look with raised eyebrows. He gave her a small nod, letting her know that he thought this was out of character for his girlfriend as well.

"Let's go," he said. "Em, love, if you need me, I'll be inside."

Emma's face softened for just a moment as she met his concerned gaze. "Thanks." She glanced at Lindsey. "Sorry, it's just . . ." She waved her hand at the crime scene, and Lindsey nodded. She understood. She did. There was a murder to investigate, and Emma didn't have time to worry about everyone's feelings.

"No problem," she said.

She and Robbie were around the corner of the building when Robbie leaned in close and said, "You need to text Sully and tell him to get here immediately."

"Okay." Lindsey frowned. "But why?"

They paused by the front door, and Lindsey used her key to unlock the automatic door and manually push it open. They stepped inside, and she closed it and locked it. They had ten more minutes until the library was officially open, which gave her just a few minutes to call the mayor's office and tell him what had happened.

"What do you know about firearms?" he asked.

"Beyond point and shoot?" she said. "Not much."

"Well, I do," he said. "My sidekick in an episode of the *Masterpiece Mystery!* series I did was a former U.S. naval officer. Our props team had to research what sort of weapon a former navy man would carry."

"Not really following," Lindsey said as she waved at Ms. Cole, who was setting up the circulation desk, while they made their way back to her office.

"Sully is former navy—am I right?" he asked.

"Yes," she said. "He left the service several years ago."

She flipped on the light switch in her office and moved to sit behind her desk. Robbie dropped into the seat across from her.

"When a navy man leaves the service, he takes his weapon with him," Robbie said. "The gun that Kirkland found was a SIG Sauer P226, which is standard issue for navy personnel. I remember the weapon from the show. It was a major plot point since only specially trained officers carry firearms in the U.K."

"What are you saying?"

"I'm saying that if that's the murder weapon, and I believe it is, then as a former navy man who was likely issued a SIG Sauer, Sully just became the prime suspect," Robbie said.

8

Lindsey was rattled. It wasn't Sully. She knew that all the way to the marrow of her bones. Despite his military background, Sully wasn't a killer. A sailor, sure, but not a killer. It had to be a weird coincidence that the gun was the murder weapon, or maybe it had been back there behind the bushes coincidentally. Highly unlikely, but she wasn't above clinging to even that sliver of hope.

Over the next couple of hours, she and Robbie took turns popping out the back door to see whether Emma and the investigators were still there. They were. Even though Grady's body had been taken to the medical examiner's office, the crime scene techs were examining every inch of the area. Emma had left to go talk to Sylvia Grady, but she came back quickly, not finding her at home.

Lindsey called Sully and told him about Grady. She didn't tell him about the gun. He was mostly concerned about whether she was okay, and when she tried to pin him down about his morning, he was interrupted by one of the passengers asking about a rock formation on one of the islands. He told her he loved her and that he'd be there as soon as he could. The wait was excruciating.

Robbie went back out to check in with Emma, and Lindsey tried to do the routine tasks her job required. She had to go over the maintenance budget, as she needed to start looking at replacing the carpet in the building. The existing industrial flooring was becoming worn, and she'd finally wrangled a commitment to replace it from the mayor. Of course, after she'd told him about Grady this morning, she sensed she had slid down the list of his favorite department heads. She was probably hovering somewhere above Parks and Recreation, because they overspent their budget every season, but she was definitely below the Water Department. Mayor Hensen loved them since they were a never-ending, never-fluctuating revenue stream for the town.

She had just started going over her spending spreadsheets when Sully popped his head into her office.

"Hey, darlin', you busy?" he asked.

The summer sun had left its mark upon him, bleaching the hair on his forearms and on his head with strands of pure gold while it bronzed his skin a rich brown. He looked windswept and smelled of the sea. Lindsey jumped up from her desk and hustled around it to hug him tight.

"Hey there," he said. He kissed her head and hugged her back. "It'll be all right. I know it had to be upsetting finding him like that, but given his behavior, he may have been harassing someone else who decided to take matters into their own hands. Em will figure it out. I'm sure of it."

"No, it's not that," Lindsey said. "They found the murder weapon, or what we assume is the weapon. It was near his body, tossed into the bushes."

"What? That's crazy. What if a kid had found it?"

"Exactly," Lindsey said. "See? You think just like I do. You would never leave a gun out in the open."

"Of course not," he said. "Wait." He pulled back to look at her. "What do you mean '*you* would never leave a gun out in the open'? You don't think I did this, do you?"

"No!" she said. "But the weapon . . ."

"Is a SIG Sauer P226," Emma said from behind Sully. "And I believe as a retired naval officer, you probably have one."

Sully turned to look at Emma. He met her gaze without flinching. Lindsey felt her heart pound in her chest. It was ridiculous. There was no way Sully would ever shoot anyone unless he had to, and that was not the case here.

"Is it the murder weapon?" he asked.

"Don't know yet," Emma said. "We'll have to wait until the ballistics report comes in. Do you have your service revolver in your possession?"

123

"Of course I do," Sully said. He looked annoyed. "I keep it in my office on the pier, locked in the safe."

"Then you won't mind retrieving it for me," Emma said.

"Not at all," he said.

"Wait," Lindsey said. "Maybe you should have a lawyer present or at least have a warrant delivered first."

They all turned to look at her, but she had no interest in anyone's reaction except Sully's. He gave her a small smile. "Don't worry. My gun is safely locked away. I can show it to Emma, and that should clear me of suspicion." He gave Emma a questioning glance.

"It will certainly help," she said.

"Let's go," Sully said.

Emma and Sully turned to leave, and Lindsey followed. There was no way she was letting Sully do this on his own. She grabbed her purse out of her desk and followed them. Pausing by the circulation desk, Lindsey told Ms. Cole she'd be right back. Surprisingly, the lemon simply nodded, and Lindsey realized she must look more stressed than she'd thought.

"It'll be all right," Paula said from beside Ms. Cole.

That clinched it. Lindsey took a deep breath and forced a small smile. "Call me if you need me."

The two women nodded, and Lindsey saw Robbie waiting for them by the front door. He fell into step beside Emma and Lindsey joined Sully as they all stepped out into the hot sticky July day.

Because the pier was within walking distance, the four of them crossed the main road, cut through the town park and walked down the pier until they reached the small office where Sully ran his water-taxi and boat-tour company.

Ronnie, his octogenarian office manager, was sitting at her desk, filing her purple nails. Her cranberry red hair was piled up on top of her head in its usual ball-shaped bun. Her jewelry, circa the nineteen seventies, included strings of big white round plastic beads at her throat and right wrist, with matching earrings and a ring on her left index finger. The look reminded Lindsey of Wilma Flintstone, but she was smart enough not to say anything.

At the sight of the four of them, Ronnie lowered her nail file and stared at them over her rhine-stone encrusted cat's-eye reading glasses. She glanced from Sully to Emma and back. "What gives?"

"Nothing much," Sully said. "I just need to get something out of the safe."

Ronnie narrowed her eyes. "Okay."

She scooted out of her chair and made room for him. The safe was built into the wall behind

Ronnie's desk. Sully hunched down and turned the combination lock on the safe. It clicked, and he twisted the handle on the safe and pulled the heavy door open. He reached inside and pulled out another metal box. This one was also locked. He retrieved a set of keys from the safe and used them to open the box. When he popped the lid, they all leaned forward. The box was empty.

Sully's head snapped up, and he met Lindsey's gaze. "I didn't."

"I know." She saw the look of shocked bewilderment on his face and knew even more certainly than before that he was innocent.

She turned to Emma. The chief looked upset. Lindsey knew what she was going to say next.

"I'm sorry, Sully. I'm going to have to take you in for further questioning," Emma said.

"What is going on?" Ronnie asked. Her gaze darted to all their faces, as if she could read the answer there.

"It's just a formality, Ronnie," Sully said. "There's been a shooting, and Emma has to track down any leads, of which I am now one."

"But that's ridiculous," Lindsey said. "Obviously, if Sully had shot Aaron Grady with his own gun, he wouldn't have volunteered to open up his safe to you. Come on, Emma—you know this is a setup."

"I'm sorry—" Emma began, but Ronnie interrupted.

"Aaron Grady was shot?" she asked.

"Yes, this morning," Robbie answered. "Outside the library."

"Well, that's easy to clear up," Ronnie said. "Sully was here with me, setting up for the tour this morning."

"What time?" Emma asked. Her gaze stayed on Sully's face.

"Seven o'clock, the usual," Ronnie said.

"What time did you leave your house, Sully?" Emma asked. Her voice was even, betraying nothing of what she was feeling.

"Six fifteen, same as every day," he said.

"Can anyone account for your whereabouts between six fifteen and seven?"

Sully shook his head. "No." He turned to Ronnie and said, "Call Charlie Peyton, and see if he can take over my tours for the rest of the day."

Ronnie nodded. Her big beads bobbled as she did so, and Lindsey got the feeling she was trying not to cry. She underestimated Ronnie. When the feisty lady stepped back around her desk and picked up her phone, her cheeks had two spots of red, and there was a fire in her eyes that looked as if it could burn through steel.

"Don't you worry, boss," she said. "I'll take care of things here, and I'll plan your jailbreak if I have to."

Sully grinned.

"Um . . . police chief . . . standing right here," Emma said.

Ronnie turned her fiery gaze on her. "Then consider yourself warned."

Lindsey felt her panic wan. Ronnie was right. There was no need to be worried; they would fight for Sully if they had to, and they would win.

The police station was in chaos when they arrived. Sylvia Grady was pacing in front of the desk officer, a rookie named Harrison, demanding to speak to Emma, when they pushed open the door and strode in.

"Chief Plewicki, what is going on?" Sylvia demanded. "I got your voice mail and had to leave a very important work conference to come here, but no one will tell me anything."

"Right, if I could have a word with you alone, Mrs. Grady," she said. She went to take Sylvia's arm, but the woman snatched it away.

"No, tell me now. What is happening?" Sylvia glanced from Emma to Robbie, Sully and then Lindsey. "You! This has something to do with you, doesn't it?"

Lindsey didn't know what to say. She shook her head, not wanting to escalate the situation but not wanting to assume any responsibility for what Emma was about to say either.

"Mrs. Grady, please calm down," Emma said. Her voice was stern. It was a tone that didn't allow for argument. "I will speak with you in private, or you can wait here until I am done with other matters."

Sylvia studied her face. Emma didn't give an inch, and the woman relented. "Fine."

"I'll be right back," Emma said to them. Then she turned to Sylvia. "Please follow me."

Emma led her back to her office. Lindsey, Sully and Robbie waited in tense silence with Officer Harrison. The ticking of the clock was the loudest noise in the room, until there was an anguished cry breaking the quiet. Lindsey felt the hair on her arms stand up.

"Maybe you all should wait in the break room," Harrison said. He was tall and lanky, a fresh graduate out of the police academy, and he looked like he wanted to escape the room with them. So he was smart, too.

"Excellent notion," Robbie said. He gestured for Lindsey and Sully to follow him toward a room in the opposite direction of Emma's office. They got only a few steps before the door to Emma's office flew open and slammed into the wall.

"You!" Sylvia flew across the lobby at Sully. "You did this. You killed my husband."

Sully held up his hands to ward her off. Lindsey moved to stand in front of him as if to protect him from the enraged woman. It was a bad move, as the sight of Lindsey made her even angrier.

"He did it for you, didn't he?" Sylvia roared. "He murdered my husband for you."

"Oy, and we were so close," Robbie said.

"No, he didn't," Lindsey argued. "Sully would never harm anyone."

"Liar!" Sylvia cried. Her face was red, and tears were coursing down her cheeks. "You flaunted yourself in front of my Aaron and turned his head. This is your fault. My love, my life, my Aaron, would still be alive if it wasn't for you. You home-wrecker!"

"That's enough!" Sully snapped. Lindsey hadn't known him when he was in the military, but the command in his voice reminded her that he had been an officer; he knew how to lead and give orders, and he didn't suffer slander—not from anyone. "I'm sorry for your loss, ma'am, but no one here is to blame. None of us had anything to do with your husband's murder."

Sylvia blinked at him. She studied him as if she was reconsidering what she'd originally thought about him. Lindsey held her breath. Was the woman going to have another fit? She didn't. Instead, her look of grief was replaced by one that was calculating.

"Then why are you here?" she asked.

There it was. The fact was that it looked very bad for Sully. A gun had been found near Grady, the same gun Sully owned. The odds that it was the murder weapon were not in their favor, and if Sylvia knew this, she would shout it from the rooftops, and there wouldn't be a thing Sully or Lindsey could do about it.

"I found the body," Robbie said. "That's why we're here. I felt the need to have my friends with me for moral support."

He stepped forward, using his movie-star good looks, his British sensibility and his calm demeanor to disarm Sylvia. It worked.

"You did?" she asked. She turned to him, and her expression crumpled. She looked as if she was about to burst into tears, and Robbie opened his arms to hug her and let her cry it out all over him.

"Oh my God." She sobbed into his shoulder. "Was it awful? Did he say anything? Did he look like he suffered?"

"There, there," Robbie said. "Let's get you a nice cup of tea, and I'll tell you everything."

Emma frowned and he shrugged. She waved him toward her office, and they watched as Robbie escorted Sylvia back across the station. When the door shut behind them, Emma faced Sully.

"I'm going to have to keep you here until the state investigator shows up," she said. "They're going to want to interview you. In the meantime, I'll need a formal statement from both of you and Robbie, too."

"Are you arresting Sully?" Lindsey asked.

"No," Emma said. "Not yet."

"You know I didn't do this," he said.

"I know," Emma said. "But someone has gone to an awful lot of trouble to make it look as if you did. Why?"

Sully shrugged.

"I don't want to do anything to compromise this investigation, so I'm sorry, but you are a person of interest until further notice," Emma said.

She glanced between them as if expecting an argument. There was none to be made. They both knew that as maddening as it was, following procedure was the best defense for now. Emma led them into a back room that had a squashy couch, a TV and a water cooler.

"Wait here," she said.

When she returned, she handed them the Briar Creek Police Department voluntary-statement forms, with which Lindsey was sadly all too familiar.

"I'm going to send Robbie back here to fill one out, too," she said. "Maybe between the three of you, we can get a clue as to what is happening. Have Officer Harrison come get me if you need me."

When she left, Lindsey dropped her form onto the table and hugged Sully. She needed to comfort and be comforted, but mostly she needed to know that everything was going to be all right.

"I hate this," she said.

"I know." He ran his hand up and down her back. He leaned back and studied her face and gave her a small smile. "You don't doubt me for a second, do you?"

"Never," she said. "I know you're innocent, absolutely positively."

His smile turned into a grin. "Well, I can't ask for more than that out of the future Mrs. Sullivan, now can I?"

This time Lindsey grinned, and for the first time, she felt a spark of optimism. She kissed him.

"Oh, bugger it, get a room," Robbie teased as he joined them.

Sully and Lindsey broke apart, but Lindsey didn't step away. She glanced at Robbie. "How is she?"

"Still crying," he said. "But she's calmed down quite a bit."

"Thanks for your help," Sully said. "You were a champ to jump in there."

"No problem, mate," Robbie said. He punched Sully on the arm. "I know you'd do the same for me."

Sully studied his longtime rival, and then he punched him back. "Absolutely, I would."

Lindsey glanced between them. "Are you two becoming friends?"

"God, no," Robbie protested. "We're mates. That's totally different and much more meaningful."

"Whatever you say," Lindsey said. Still, she could tell that their adversarial relationship had changed somewhere along the line, and she was delighted.

She handed Robbie his form, and the three of them sat down to fill them out. They didn't compare their information, knowing that they would all remember different aspects of the morning.

When they were finished, Robbie glanced up and said, "Emma told me you're staying here to talk to the state investigators."

"That's right," Sully said.

"I'll shadow Lindsey for the rest of the day," Robbie said. "Whoever shot Grady is still at large, and who knows what their game is."

"Thanks," Sully said. "That will make staying here a whole lot easier." He turned to Lindsey. "You're going to have to be as careful now as you were when it was Grady following you, possibly even more so. There's a reason he was shot and killed outside the library, and you won't be safe until we know who did it and why."

9

Lindsey hated leaving Sully at the police station. He wasn't locked up, but that was cold comfort. The gun being the same model as his and his service revolver having gone missing were coincidences that were impossible to ignore. She tried not to fret, but it certainly appeared that someone was trying to make Sully look guilty. It had to be someone who was out to get Grady, who knew that she and Sully had had altercations with both Gradys the night before at the Blue Anchor.

"Where to now?" Robbie asked as they exited the police station. "Back to work? Or do you want to go home and call it a day?"

"Neither," Lindsey said. "I want to go back to Sully's office."

Robbie raised one pale eyebrow.

"I know they have a security camera that records the exterior of the building and the boats," she said. "It could be that whoever broke into the office and stole his gun is on that footage."

"Good thinking," he said. "Don't you think Emma will want the footage?"

"Yes," Lindsey said. "Which is why I want to go there and review it first."

He groaned. "She is going to be so unhappy about this."

Lindsey nodded. "True, but look at it this way. If we look at it first and find something, we are saving her so much time, and then she can get on with chasing down whoever we find on the video. Really, we're doing a public service."

"Well, when you put it like that, how could we not?" Robbie said. He rolled a hand in the direction of the door. "Lead on."

When they arrived at the boat-tour office, Ian Murphy was there. He was reviewing some paperwork with Ronnie, and they both glanced up when Lindsey and Robbie entered. The disappointment on their faces made it clear that they had been hoping for Sully.

"Is he under arrest?" Ian asked. He'd been partners with Sully in the boat-tour business before he'd opened the restaurant with Mary and he still participated in the business.

"No," Lindsey said. "But he's definitely a person of interest because of the weapon found near the body. Emma's keeping him, as she wants him to talk to the state investigators."

"I say we take his truck and drive it right through the side of the jail," Ronnie said. "We should just bust him out, get him a bogus passport and send him out of the country."

"That's it, no more Tom Cruise *Mission: Impossible* movies for you," Ian said. Then he smiled at her as if he could picture her doing exactly what she'd said. Lindsey could, too, and it did not reassure her.

"What can we do to help?" Ian asked.

"Let me review the video from your security camera," she said. "I know it monitors the exterior of the building and the boats. Maybe we can see who sneaked into the office and stole Sully's gun."

Ian shook his head. "I have no idea how to work that thing. Charlie is our guy for the high-tech security stuff, and he's out on the water, since he stepped in to take Sully's next tour. He won't be back for at least an hour."

"The police might arrive wanting the video by then," Robbie said.

"You mean they'll come by and ask if we have a security camera?" Ronnie asked. She looked at Ian and said, "That's simple. My mama always said when you want to avoid something, play dumb. 'Security camera? Do we have a security camera?'"

Robbie gave her a small smile. "I see you've got some acting chops."

Ronnie nodded. "You don't make it into your eighties without learning how to improvise."

"I have to take the water taxi out to make some deliveries, and I need to pick up Piper Meadows on Horseshoe Island, so I won't be here," Ian said. "Can you handle the police if they come, or would you rather close for the day?"

Ronnie gave him a look that would have withered any man with less of a backbone. "I've got this. Don't worry that pretty little head of yours."

Ian grinned and glanced back at Lindsey and Robbie. "All right. As soon as Charlie gets in, I'll have him deal with the security camera, and we'll be in touch."

"Thanks," Lindsey said. She glanced back at Ronnie. "Please be careful. Whoever did this is still at large. If they discover there's a security system in place here, they may come around trying to destroy any evidence."

Ronnie gave her a blank look. "What security system?"

Lindsey laughed. She had no doubt Ronnie could fool someone with her blank expression, but it was still worrisome.

"Don't worry," Ian said. "I'll push back my run to the islands until Charlie gets here so she isn't alone, and I'll stay out of sight if the police happen by."

Ronnie gave him an exasperated look, but she didn't argue.

Lindsey and Robbie left the office and made

their way back to the library. Lindsey was surprised at Robbie's silence. He usually had something to say no matter what the circumstances. She glanced at him and saw frown lines bracketing his mouth.

"What are you thinking?" she asked.

"That it's highly unlikely that—what do you Americans say?—that this was Grady's first rodeo," he said. "Every time I've had a stalker who was a significant problem, there was always a victim before me," Robbie said. "The last one I had was trying to recover from her obsession with Hugh Grant by focusing on me. I like to think I was a step up for her, but I imagine Hugh would argue with that."

"You think Grady has stalked women before?" Lindsey asked.

"Seems likely," Robbie said. "He zeroed in on you so fast, and he clearly didn't think there was anything wrong with his behavior. I'm betting if we dig, we'll find other victims in his past."

"And it could be one of them who took the opportunity to kill him," Lindsey said. She snapped her fingers. "That's brilliant."

Robbie puffed out his chest. "I know." Then he sobered. "Where do we start? I suppose I could talk to his wife."

"I think we need to stay clear of her," Lindsey said. "Regardless of our feelings about Grady, she's grieving, plus you're dating the chief of police. No matter how you approach it, that doesn't look good."

"Agreed," Robbie said. "You said his hobby was growing roses. Don't we have a local gardening club? He might have gotten connected with them. Maybe he talked about you or his wife or developed another obsession."

"I did refer him to the local group," Lindsey said. "I have the names and numbers of the officers at the reference desk."

"Let's go," Robbie said.

When they walked through the front doors of the library, Lindsey immediately scanned the room, looking for Aaron Grady. She hadn't realized how jumpy she had become until she remembered that he was never going to sit in this building and stare at her again. She was flooded with relief and then felt horribly guilty. The man was dead, and even though he wouldn't be there to stalk her anymore, she couldn't be grateful that he had been murdered.

She stopped by the circulation desk and checked in with Ms. Cole. "Everything all right?"

Ms. Cole studied her over the top edge of her reading glasses. "It's just as it should be. Are you all right?"

"Getting there," Lindsey said.

Ms. Cole must have sensed how unsettled Lindsey was, because she nodded and said, "We have things under control out here. Why don't you take some time to yourself."

"Thank you," Lindsey said. "I've got some calls to make, and that would be very helpful."

"Right then," Robbie said. "I'll just go make us some tea."

Lindsey thought that was the best idea she'd heard all day. "Put mine on ice, would you?"

Robbie gave her a look, but Lindsey didn't care. It was still scorchingly hot outside, and she felt as if she were melting. There was no way she was drinking anything with a temperature below icy cold.

"Savage," Robbie muttered. He strode toward the staff break room, which had a small kitchenette that he was overly familiar with for a nonemployee.

Lindsey stopped by the reference desk and plucked the card for the gardening club off the Rolodex they still maintained for local numbers. Then she made for her office. She booted up her computer and checked the listing she had bookmarked for local community organizations.

The Briar Creek Garden Club had a bare-bones website. It showed the date and time of the next meeting, a photo album of members' gardens and a list of the group officers, which matched the one Lindsey already had. There wasn't much to it, which was most likely because the dissemination of information happened in their monthly meetings rather than online. She found a newsletter link and clicked on it. She opened the latest one and discovered that it had all sorts of tips for dealing with the drought. Good to know.

She scrolled all the way to the last page, scanning the letter from the president, the gardening tips and *bingo,* the new-member introductions. She looked at the profiles, half hoping, half dreading that she would find him listed there. Halfway through the list of seven new members, there he was. In his picture, he wore the same closed-lip smirk she remembered and it made her skin crawl.

Grady. What had been his damage, anyway? She read through his bio. It said that after a long career with Berkshire County in the budget office, he had retired to spend his time cultivating roses. At his wife's request, they had moved to Connecticut. He'd been married to Sylvia for twenty-eight years, and they hoped to travel the world together after she retired.

They sounded like a perfectly nice and normal couple, but when Lindsey looked at his photo, she didn't think he looked nice. Rather, he looked creepy and a bit scary.

Robbie entered her office, carrying a mug of hot tea for himself and a glass of iced tea for her. He looked over her shoulder and read the short bio next to Grady's photo.

"He's got crazy eyes, doesn't he?" he asked.

Lindsey toasted him with her glass. "Thank you. I thought it was just me."

"What have you discovered about him?"

"That he and Sylvia recently moved here from Tollenton, Massachusetts," she said. She paused to sip her iced tea before she opened a new window on her computer and searched for garden clubs in and around Tollenton. It was a small town on the edge of the Berkshires. The town website made it look like an ideal village with a large town green and a river running through the center of what looked like a picturesque village. When Lindsey refined her search to add roses specifically as a subject of interest, it brought up several listings, but the one that caught her attention was the Berkshire Rose Club. She clicked on the "Contact Us" tab and picked up her phone.

Robbie sipped his tea, watching Lindsey over the rim while he listened.

"Hello, you've reached Trudy Glass, the president of the Berkshire Rose Club. I'm unable to take your call right now, but if you leave your name and number, I'll get back to you as soon as I can," a pleasant voice said.

"Hi," Lindsey said. "My name is Lindsey Norris, and I'm calling for some information about your gardening club. If you could return my call, I would really appreciate it." She left her number and hung up, feeling as if the tiny trail she had been following had grown cold.

"Don't fret," Robbie said. "She'll call back. In the meantime, so long as you stay safely here in your office, I'll go around to our local gardening club and see if anyone has anything to say about Grady. Who knows, maybe he got into a fight with one of them about aphids, and we'll have a new suspect."

"Good idea," Lindsey said. "I think I need to tell our parents what's happening."

"Your parents are still visiting his parents?"

"Yes, in fact, they're headed back to New Hampshire tomorrow. I hate to ruin their last night on the island," she said.

"Then don't," Robbie said. "Listen, we both know Emma isn't going to keep Sully a second longer than necessary. I bet as soon as the state investigators finish with him, she releases him."

"I'd agree except for the gun," Lindsey said. "If the one they found is Sully's . . ."

"It might not be," Robbie said. "This is a boating community. There are loads of former navy men around here."

"Yes, but how many of them had a public argument with Grady?" she asked.

"There's that logical librarian mind again," Robbie said. "There's no talking to you when you're like this. I still say you should wait before you tell your parents. See if Sully is let out tonight or not."

"All right, I'll bend to your optimism." Lindsey

gave him a half smile. She turned back to her desk and then glanced at the clock. "I'm going to have to work late tonight to make up for the time I missed today. Meet me here later after you do gardener recon?"

"Of course," Robbie said. He finished his tea and rose from his seat. He glanced down at Lindsey and said, "Be careful, pet. When I say don't leave your office, I mean it. There's a killer out there, and until we know who it is and why they shot Grady, you're not safe."

"I know," she said. She gestured to her desk. "With all my work piling up, I doubt I'll be able to leave my office today."

"Probably for the best," he said. "And just in case, I'll have Charlie Peyton pop in to keep an eye on you."

He left with a wave, and Lindsey reached for her phone but then stopped. She wanted to call Sully to see whether he was still at the police station, but she didn't. He would be in touch as soon as he could, and pestering him with phone calls probably wouldn't help.

Instead, she opened up her email and began to answer the messages that had piled up while she was gone. The town had implemented a new customer service model, and Lindsey needed to figure out how to get her staff trained over at the town hall and still have enough coverage to run the library. She wondered whether she could send two staff members and have them come back and train the rest of her employees. She looked at the calendar and noticed with summer vacations in full swing, they were operating with a skeleton crew as it was.

At the thought of a skeleton, her mind flitted back to finding Grady's body outside the building. She thought about Robbie's theory that he had stalked other women, and even though she didn't wish that awfulness on anyone, she was hoping it was true so that they had a bigger pool of suspects to choose from, because there was no denying that at the moment, Sully was the most likely suspect, even though she knew he wasn't guilty and she knew Emma knew it, too.

She sipped her iced tea, noting the condensation on the glass left a small puddle on the tile coaster on her desk. She wondered when this horrible drought would end. She did a quick check of the weather app on her cell phone and noted there was nothing but sunshine predicted for the next week. She realized she was restless, and knew that the odds of getting any meaningful work done while Sully was still at the police station were slim to none.

Her phone rang, startling her out of her brooding. She picked it up, bracing herself for the possibility that it was a reporter. She had politely declined to comment when they'd called earlier that morning, and she was holding firm to that decision even though a few of them had been spotted outside the building. So far she'd been lucky that they were more interested in hanging around the police station.

"Hello, Briar Creek Public Library, may I help you?" she answered on the second ring.

"Hi, my name is Trudy Glass, and I'm returning a call from a Lindsey Norris," a woman said.

"Hi, Ms. Glass, this is Lindsey," she said. "Thanks for returning my call."

"Call me Trudy, please, and it was no trouble," she said. "Are you interested in membership?"

"Actually, I'm calling from Connecticut," Lindsey said. "I'm a public librarian here, and I was looking for some information."

"Oh, all right, how can I help you?"

"I was wondering what you could tell me about one of your former members, Aaron Grady?" Lindsey asked.

"Aaron?" Trudy asked. "Why, he left us several months ago. Is everything all right?"

"I'm sorry to say no," Lindsey said. "Mr. Grady was shot and killed early this morning."

Trudy gasped. "That's awful. Was it a robbery?"

"We don't know," Lindsey said. "I'm calling because, well, frankly we were wondering if there was anyone in the rose club up there who might have had an issue with Mr. Grady."

"But didn't you say you're at the library? Are

you a concerned friend of his?" Trudy asked. "Is that why you're calling?"

Lindsey blanched at the thought of being friends with Grady. The man had made the past few weeks miserable and not a little scary. Still, going along with it was probably the best way to get information, so she decided to neither confirm nor deny.

"I am definitely concerned," she said. This was one hundred percent true. "Which is why I'm calling. He was new to Briar Creek, so it seems unlikely that it was someone here. It made me wonder if there was anyone from his prior residence who had an issue with him."

"I don't think so," Trudy said. She sounded truly mystified. "He was always personable. Showed up for the meetings on time, helped out with the fund-raisers—you know, just a pleasant man who kept to himself quite a bit, but most gardeners are introverts. We are happiest when we're outdoors with the sun on our face and our clippers in hand."

Lindsey thought of Grady wielding clippers, and the image terrified her. But Grady had been shot—not a gardener's first choice of weapon, Lindsey was guessing. She thought a solid whack with a hoe to the back of the head would be more likely, or perhaps a shanking with a pair of shears.

"You know who you should talk to?" Trudy said.

"No, who?"

"Chloe Weber," she said. "She interviewed Aaron for a piece in the newspaper. They seemed to form a fast friendship, but then after the article came out, they had a falling out. One of our members saw Chloe in the grocery store, and she was very upset about Aaron. When I asked him about it, Aaron said she was mad that he had critiqued her article for the paper. He said she was touchy."

"And which paper would that be?" Lindsey asked. She had the feeling it wasn't just that Chloe was touchy.

"Oh, this was for the local *Berkshire Day*," she said. "It was a very big deal at the time. Chloe followed Aaron around for a couple of weeks, and then she just vanished. Aaron said she was on to her next assignment. He said her article about him and his roses raised her profile enough to get a job at a larger newspaper. Isn't that wonderful?"

"And her name was Chloe Weber?" Lindsey grabbed a pen and wrote the name down. "When did that article get printed?"

"About a year ago," Trudy said. She sounded as if she wasn't sure. "No, wait—it was more than that. The article ran in June of last year, so about a year and a month."

"Thank you, Trudy, you've been very helpful," Lindsey said. "If you think of anything else or anyone else who might have more information about Aaron, please don't hesitate to call me."

"I will," Trudy said. "You know, it's such a shame. Aaron really did grow the most marvelous roses. Why, he had a Jude the Obscure, a fabulous peach-tinted rose, that was so round and fat with petals, you'd think it was a peony." She sighed, and there was a slight hesitation in her voice when she added, "You know, there were some members of the rose club who didn't care for Aaron."

"Really?" Lindsey asked. She tried to sound encouraging.

"I hesitate to say anything, as I don't like to gossip, but there was some bad blood about that article Ms. Weber wrote," Trudy said. "Some of the club members felt that Aaron was pushy and that he monopolized her, making his garden the centerpiece of an article that was supposed to be about the whole club."

"When you say he monopolized her, what do you mean exactly?" Lindsey asked. She felt her body grow tense. Could Aaron have been stalking Chloe Weber? And if so, how had that turned out? Maybe there was a police report.

"Oh, you know, she'd come to the meetings, and he'd greet her with big bouquets of roses from his garden," Trudy said. "Some members felt that he was showing off and trying to impress her to make sure she wrote mostly about him."

Roses. He had brought her roses. Lindsey

felt her heart speed up in her chest. Had Aaron been watching Chloe like he'd been watching Lindsey? Had Chloe reported it? Maybe there was a record of it. Maybe there were even more women he had done this to. Lindsey forced her voice to remain calm and conversational.

"Was that it?" Lindsey asked. "What I mean is, was he only interested in her because of the article, or do you think he was interested in her as a person?"

"I . . . well . . . I'm not sure," Trudy said. "I mean, he's—he was—married. I thought he was only interested in making sure that Chloe wrote a positive piece about the club, but the last time I saw her, she said something that I found odd."

"What was that?" Lindsey asked.

"I ran into her in the post office, and she was filling out a change-of-address slip," Trudy said. "I assumed she was moving because she'd gotten a new job as Aaron had said, but when I asked about it, she said, 'To put it in gardener speak, sometimes an invasive weed can't be eradicated, and the only way to keep gardening is to find a new plot of land.'"

"What did you think of that?" Lindsey asked.

"I thought maybe she was unhappy at work or had a bad relationship," Trudy said. "I didn't think it had anything to do with Aaron Grady, but perhaps I was wrong. She left shortly after the article came out, and Aaron left the rose club a few weeks after that." She lowered her voice to a whisper, clearly uncomfortable with gossiping. "Do you suppose they had an affair and it went wrong?"

"I don't know," Lindsey said. She doubted it was an affair. She had a feeling Aaron had driven Chloe away from her life, forcing her to flee to put some distance between her and him, just like Lindsey had been contemplating taking a new job when she thought she'd have to put up with him staring at her. Had Chloe tried to escape him? There was only one way to find out. She was going to have to follow this clue.

"Trudy, you don't happen to have a phone number for Chloe Weber, do you?"

10

"Did the reporter call back?" Robbie asked. He had finished talking to all the local garden club members that he could find and was sitting back in the chair opposite Lindsey's desk while they compared what they'd been able to uncover about Aaron Grady.

"No, the number was disconnected," Lindsey said. "But I asked Charlene La Rue to use her journalist contacts to see if anyone at the TV station has heard of Chloe." Violet's daughter, Charlene, was also a crafternooner, as well as a television reporter in New Haven. "It's a long shot, but I've checked all of the directories I can think of in-house. What about the garden club? Any leads?"

"No one liked him, if that's what you mean," Robbie said. "Apparently, he exuded an arrogant yet needy vibe that was off-putting to the membership."

"Sounds about right," Lindsey said. She kept one eye on her computer, watching the database run the name Chloe Weber. "The rose club in Massachusetts had similar issues with him."

"Any word on Water Boy?" Robbie asked. "Is

he going to be allowed to leave the station?"

"Yes, in fact, he texted a little while ago that he expected to be out in time for dinner," she said. "We're going to head over to the Blue Anchor. Want to join us?"

"No, thanks," Robbie said. "The third wheel is always the squeakiest."

Lindsey was about to protest that he wasn't a third wheel, but he held up his hand and said, "I'm going to pop in at the station and force Emma to eat some dinner. Maybe we'll see you there, although knowing her, I'll only be able to get her to slow down enough for a gourmet meal of Cheez-Its and Twix bars from the vending machine in the break room."

"Well, that does cover all of the food groups," Lindsey said. "You know, salty and sweet."

Robbie smiled, but Lindsey's phone rang, cutting off anything she would have said. She picked up, hoping it was Charlene. It was.

"Hello—"

"Lindsey, hey, I have to be on set in five minutes for the early news," Charlene said. "Here's what I've got. No one at the station had heard of Chloe Weber, so I reached out to some print-journalist friends at the *Register*, and sure enough, one of them went to journalism school with her."

"Are they still in contact?"

"They weren't, but Chloe recently reached out, looking for work. She's been freelancing for the

Associated Press but under a different name. She writes under the name Amanda Morgan for them as well as for some other small papers around the country."

"That's weird, isn't it?" Lindsey asked. "I mean, it's not like she's a novelist needing a pen name."

"Some journalists who work freelance take on multiple names so they can have many stories in print papers and online to increase their income streams," Charlene said. "This is not a business a person goes into because they're going to get rich."

"Huh, I never knew that," Lindsey said. "Do you have a number for her?"

"I do, but promise me you won't share it," Charlene said. "My friend said Chloe is hyper-vigilant about maintaining her privacy. Also, they asked that you not divulge who gave you her number. Grab a pen."

Charlene read the number, and Lindsey jotted the numbers down on an old envelope.

"Got it," Lindsey said. "Thanks, Charlene, you're the best."

"Yes, yes, I'm coming," Charlene replied to some mumbled voice in the background. "See you at crafternoon next week."

"Great, okay, bye," Lindsey said. "And thanks."

She hung up, and Robbie waited with one eyebrow quirked up in inquiry. "Well?"

155

"Chloe Weber has been a freelance writer working under the name Amanda Morgan," she said. She went back to the database and changed her search. A flurry of articles from the *Register* and the Associated Press filled the screen. She did an image search to see whether there was a photo of Amanda Morgan, and while there were several Amanda Morgans listed—a hairstylist, a student and a teacher popped up first—there were none that matched the reporter's bio.

Lindsey picked up the phone and called the number Charlene had given her. The phone rang four times, and then voice mail picked up. The voice was a mechanical man's voice stating that Amanda was unavailable but would call back as soon as possible. Lindsey clutched the receiver. What message should she leave that would get Chloe/Amanda to call her back? She thought about pretending to be a newspaper looking to hire her, but she hated lying. She decided to go with the truth.

"Hi, Amanda, my name is Lindsey Norris, and I'm calling to talk to you about Aaron Grady. You wrote a piece about him under the name Chloe Weber—"

"Who are you?" a female voice interrupted.

Lindsey sent Robbie a surprised look. He leaned in closer so he could hear, too.

"My name is Lindsey Norris," she said. "I—"

"How did you get this number?" the woman demanded.

"I'm a librarian," Lindsey said, as if that was explanation enough. Apparently, it was.

"What do you want?"

Lindsey made her voice calm, making sure she didn't match the suspicion and hostility in Chloe's tone. "I wanted to talk to you about Aaron Grady," she said.

"Why?"

Lindsey glanced at Robbie and he nodded.

"Because he's dead," Lindsey said.

There was a gasp on the other end of the phone. A few seconds ticked by before Chloe spoke. Her voice was nervous when she said, "I don't believe you. Prove it."

"It's all over the news," Lindsey said. "He was found dead from a gunshot wound outside the Briar Creek Public Library early this morning."

"Hold on," Chloe said.

Lindsey heard the furious tapping of keys on a keyboard. There was no sound for a bit, and she wondered whether they'd been disconnected. Just when she was certain that they had, Chloe came back on the phone.

"Briar Creek?" Chloe's voice was high pitched and sounded terrified. "What was he doing in Briar Creek?"

"From what I understand, he moved here a few months ago," Lindsey said.

"Oh my God." Chloe's voice was faint. "He's been living in Briar Creek for months?"

There was a note of hysteria in her voice, and Lindsey didn't know what to say other than to confirm her question.

"From what he said, yes, I believe so," she said.

"So he followed me," Chloe said. Her voice sounded faint.

"Followed you?" Lindsey asked. "I'm not sure I understand."

"Who shot him?" Chloe asked, disregarding Lindsey's words.

"They don't know," Lindsey said. "The police are investigating."

There was silence for a moment, and then Chloe's voice when she spoke was so soft Lindsey had to strain to hear her.

"But he's definitely dead?" Chloe asked.

"Yes," Lindsey said. "I saw him myself."

There was a sigh, as if Chloe was relieved, but then her voice grew sharp and she said, "I don't understand why you're calling me."

Again, Lindsey looked at Robbie, and again, he nodded.

"The truth is, Chloe, that I was having some problems with Mr. Grady," she said. She blew out a breath. "From what I learned about his time in the Berkshire Rose Club, it occurred to me that you might have had a similar experience with him."

Again, there was silence.

"Chloe, any information you have about him could help the police solve this case," she said.

"What if I don't care?" Chloe asked.

Robbie's eyes went wide at that.

"So he did harass you," Lindsey said. "Let me guess—he brought you large bouquets of roses, showed up at your house, started following you, sent you creepy text messages?"

"Emails," Chloe said. "I got creepy emails. Pages of them. I assume he stalked you, too?"

"Yes," Lindsey said. "And now my fiancé is being questioned in his murder, and he didn't do it. I need your help, Chloe."

"I'm sorry. I can't—" she began, but Lindsey interrupted.

"If I found you, the police will, too," she said. "Don't you think it's best if you come in and talk to them voluntarily before they treat you like a suspect?"

She was absolutely bluffing, but Chloe's comment that Grady had "followed her," after Lindsey had mentioned Briar Creek, meant that she was somewhere in the area. Lindsey would knock on every door in a five-town radius if she had to, but Chloe was going to come forward.

"A suspect?" Chloe snapped. "I had nothing to do with his shooting. I left Massachusetts and came to the Thumb Islands specifically to get away from him, but he must have figured it out and followed me."

So she was on the islands. Lindsey felt her hope for Sully's freedom surge.

"Which makes you look like a suspect," Lindsey said. "Of course, if it was in self-defense—"

"I didn't shoot him," Chloe cried.

Robbie put his hand out flat in the air and lowered it, gesturing for Lindsey to take it down a notch. She nodded.

"Then come into town and talk to the police," Lindsey said. "I'll even go with you if you want, but we need any information you have."

"I can't help you," Chloe said. "I didn't even know he was here." Her voice cracked, and Lindsey imagined she was having a reaction to the news that her stalker had been living nearby for months and she'd had no idea. Lindsey couldn't fault her. She'd freak out, too.

"Which island are you on?" Lindsey asked. "I'll have my friend Charlie, who works for the water taxi, come and get you."

"That's not necessary," Chloe said. "I don't like to ride in anyone else's boat. I'll come in on my own, but I'd appreciate it if you'd meet me at the Blue Anchor, the restaurant on the pier. Say, seven o'clock?"

"That'll work," Lindsey said.

"Thank you," Chloe said.

"Sure." Lindsey hesitated but then added, "He can't hurt you anymore."

A laugh with no humor greeted her words, and Chloe said, "Back at you."

Lindsey hung up and slumped back in her seat. Robbie was studying her, and she shrugged.

"That was a bit more intense than I expected," she said.

"Sounds like this woman may have had it even worse than you from Grady," he said. "She quit her job and moved out onto an island. That's a serious escape act."

"I wonder why she didn't go to the police."

"Maybe she did. They're not all as progressive as Emma. Your own mayor wanted you to do nothing," he said.

"And some people wonder why women are fed up," Lindsey said.

"Right. That whole 'boys will be boys' is a load of rubbish," Robbie said. "As the son of a single mum who had to deal with gropers and perverts her whole working life and just smile through it or risk losing her livelihood, it makes me furious. Women are not possessions—why can't these thickheads get that?"

Lindsey smiled at her friend. "Well, at least there are men like you and Sully to make up for it. I do believe there are more good men than bad ones. It's just the bad ones get all the attention."

"And in this case, he got shot," Robbie said. "So there's that."

Lindsey studied him. "You know Emma isn't going to be happy with us for contacting a prior stalking victim of Grady's."

"I was thinking that myself," he said. "Especially if that call to Chloe makes her run again instead of, say, meeting you at the pier like she said she would. And if she was to run, it would probably entail bringing her boat in and then taking her car, assuming she has one parked in the island residents' lot by the pier."

"Are you willing to be the point man?"

"You mean to go sit in the Blue Anchor with a view of the pier and see if she does a runner?" he asked.

"Yeah," she said. She opened up a file on her computer that showed a picture of Chloe Weber when she was reporting for the *Berkshire Day*. She was younger than Lindsey by several years, and she had dark hair, so it seemed that Grady didn't have a type. But there was a sparkle in Chloe's eyes, and Lindsey guessed that she'd been friendly, just like Lindsey had been, and that had been enough to trigger Grady's interest.

"This is an older picture, and she may have cut or dyed her hair, but at least you'll have a general idea of who to look for," she said.

Robbie took a picture with his phone and said, "Got it. I'll go nurse a pint while I wait.

Meet me there at seven? I'll have Emma join us."

"Yes, unless you see Chloe making a getaway first," Lindsey said.

With a nod, Robbie hustled out of the library. Lindsey glanced at the wall clock. She had two hours to plow through as much work as she could before it was time to meet Chloe. She hoped the woman was telling the truth, and she really hoped she showed up at their appointed time. Lindsey did not want to face Emma with this information with no Chloe to show for it.

Sully arrived just as Lindsey was packing up her things. He stood in the doorway, his smile strained, and she rose from her desk to give him a hug.

"Long day?"

"And then some." His tone was rueful. He hugged her tight and then let her go. "The state investigators wanted to keep me overnight, but Emma was the voice of reason. She said the only evidence they had was the gun, which they'll have to run the serial numbers on before we know if it's mine or not, and ballistics will still have to match it to the victim. She vouched for me."

"Which was the right thing to do, since she knows you didn't do it."

"I love that there is not one bit of doubt in you," he said. His smile this time reached his eyes, and Lindsey hugged him again.

"Of course I don't doubt you," she said. "I'm going to marry you. I would never marry someone I didn't trust one hundred percent."

"Hearing that almost makes this whole long, boring day worth it."

"Almost?"

"If you had told me that without me being a suspect in a murder, the day would have been just that much better," he said.

"But it might not have meant as much."

Sully grinned. "Nah, it would have meant just as much."

Lindsey returned his smile. She couldn't help it. He was her everything.

"My parents are still with your parents on Bell Island," Lindsey said. "I'm having breakfast with them in the morning. I'm not going to tell them what's happening. I don't want them to worry if there's no need."

"Good call," Sully said. "I just got off the phone with my parents, and they were unaware of how I'd spent the day, so I decided to tell them after everything gets sorted."

Lindsey squeezed his hand in hers. They were both close to their parents, and it hurt to leave them out of this, but what could their parents do besides worry? Not a thing.

"I think that's for the best. Come on—I'll buy you dinner," she said. "Plus, there's someone I think we want to talk to. At least, I hope there is."

She grabbed her things and walked past him out the door. Sully was watching her with a concerned expression.

"Why does that sound so ominous?" he asked.

"Because you're overthinking it," she said. "It's just a lead. Potentially a very good lead but still just a lead."

He fell into step beside her as they exited the building. Lindsey waved to the staff at the circulation desk, telling them she'd see them tomorrow. She waited until they were out of earshot before she explained.

"I did some digging," she said.

"Of course you did."

The automatic doors slid open, and a wall of heat hit them in the face. Lindsey almost fell back into the building, the change from the cool temperature of the library to the hot dry air outside was so dramatic.

"When will this heat break?" she asked.

"No time soon," he said. "According to the weather forecast anyway."

"Ugh." She could feel the sweat bead up on her skin and run down her back as they crossed the street and headed toward the Blue Anchor.

"You were saying about the digging you did," he prodded.

"Sorry, the heat melted my brain." She shook her head and tried to focus. "Okay, so I thought I'd follow the botanical trail and see what sort of

165

relationship Grady had with the local gardening club in addition to the one he left behind in Massachusetts.

"I spoke with the president of the Berkshire Rose Club and discovered that Grady had been written about by a local reporter. I figured I would track her down and see what her impression of him was, especially as, according to the president of the gardening club, Grady and the reporter had had a falling out."

Sully nodded. He took her elbow as they crossed the street, keeping an eye out for cars while she talked.

"The reporter all but vanished shortly after the story ran," Lindsey said. "I called Charlene La Rue to see if she had heard of the woman in any of her journalism circles."

They paused as they stepped up onto the curb, and Lindsey turned to face him.

"Turns out she had, but the reporter is going by a different name now." Lindsey nodded when Sully frowned. "Brace yourself. It gets weirder. She lives out on one of the Thumb Islands. When I spoke with her—"

"You talked to her? Lindsey, what if she's the killer?"

"She isn't," she said. "She didn't even know Grady was dead."

"But she could have been lying," he said. He ran a hand through his hair. "I don't like this."

"Well, you're going to like it a lot less since we're on our way to meet her right now."

"What?" he cried.

"She said she would come in and meet me so we could talk," Lindsey said.

"Oh hell no," Sully said. "What if she murdered Grady? You just made yourself a loose end. She'll think she has to shoot you, too, or you might tell what you know to the police."

Lindsey shook her head. "She's not going to shoot me in the middle of the Blue Anchor. There are too many witnesses. Besides, I heard her voice when I told her about Grady. She was relieved but still scared. Whatever he did to me, he must have been ten times worse with her."

They entered the restaurant, and Sully immediately moved in front of Lindsey as if to block her from stray gunfire. Lindsey scanned the restaurant until she saw Robbie sitting at the bar one seat away from a pretty brunette, who looked to be the right age for Chloe. Robbie met Lindsey's gaze and gave her a slow nod.

"There she is," Lindsey said. She jerked her chin in the direction of the woman, and Sully's eyes narrowed. Lindsey nudged him. "Stop that. You look scary."

"Well, I did just get out of jail," he said.

Lindsey smiled. She walked toward the woman and held out her hand. "Hi, I'm Lindsey Norris."

Chloe glanced up. Her expression was guarded as she shook her hand. She took in Sully bringing up the rear and asked, "Who's that?"

"My fiancé," Lindsey said.

"I thought you said he was being questioned."

"I was. I just got released," Sully said. He held out his hand, and after a slight hesitation, Chloe shook it.

"Do you want to grab a table?" Lindsey asked. "Maybe get something to eat?"

Chloe glanced at them. "All right. Maybe that would help."

They moved toward an open table, and Robbie met Lindsey's glance. She tipped her head at the door, and he nodded. He'd keep watch for them. If Emma should come in, Lindsey wanted to give Chloe a warning. She didn't want the woman to think she was setting her up.

Belinda, the hostess, who was one of Lindsey's favorite library regulars, showed them to a table in the corner. She glanced at Lindsey as she put their menus on the table and asked, "Well?"

"No," Lindsey said.

Belinda stomped her rubber-soled shoe on the hard floor. "Why?"

"Because it hasn't been released yet," Lindsey said. "You know you're first on the waiting list. When Karen Rose's latest book drops, we'll rush it through processing for you. I promise."

"Thank you," Belinda said. "I'd hate to have to

seat you just outside the kitchen doors for the rest of your life."

"Harsh!" Lindsey said.

Belinda grinned, otherwise Lindsey might have been more concerned. She watched the hostess walk away and made a mental note to check on the new book orders.

"You really are a librarian," Chloe said.

"Yes," Lindsey said. "And I really did have a problem with Grady, too." She reached across the table and put her hand on top of Chloe's. "I'm sorry that I'm not the only one and that you had to go through it, too."

"He's . . . he was deranged," Chloe said. "No one would take me seriously. Just because he didn't threaten me with physical violence, they thought he just had a harmless crush that would go away if I stopped encouraging him. I never did that! From day one, I was like no, nope, not interested, go away, leave me alone. He simply would not hear me. It was maddening and then it got frightening."

Lindsey glanced up at Sully. Their eyes met, and she knew he was thinking the same thing she was. Grady had used his clean-cut looks and mild-mannered demeanor to terrorize women. It made her furious.

"Yes, well, I got a bit of that as well," Lindsey said. "Some utter garbage about how they couldn't infringe on his right to be in a public building and wouldn't kick him out, never mind that I work there and he was creeping me out and making me crazy."

Chloe shook her head. "The same thing happened to me. It's like no one considered him a threat because he looked so milquetoast. Let me tell you, when you come out of your house and he's standing on your front lawn, waiting for you, with his creepy face staring at you like you're his long-lost love, and you have no idea if he's going to break into your house and strangle you in your sleep, you start taking it pretty damn seriously."

Lindsey hesitated to ask her next question, but she felt it was important. "Chloe, did he ever harm you?"

"Hell no," she said. "I never let him get close enough to try. Once my creep radar went off, that was it. My lease was up on my apartment, so I looked for other work in the area. When I got hired to write for the *New Haven Register*, I moved and never looked back. The day my very first article was published, he called me. That's when I changed my pen name, changed my phone number and moved out to the island. I didn't hear from him again, but somehow he must have known I was here. Don't you think? It's too much of a coincidence that he moved to Briar Creek, too."

"I think he must have, but you never heard from him?" Lindsey asked.

"No," she said.

"Maybe that's why he fixated on you, Lindsey," Sully said. "Maybe being on the island made Chloe untouchable, so he switched his attention to you."

"If that's the case, I'm sorry," Chloe said. "I wouldn't wish that living nightmare on anyone."

"There's no need—it's not your fault. Do you know what triggered his interest in you?" Lindsey asked.

"The article—" Chloe began, but the waitress arrived to take their order.

Sully and Lindsey went with the house special, which was a stuffed broiled cod, and Chloe ordered fried clams. As soon as the waitress left, Chloe continued.

"When I went to the first meeting of the Berkshire Rose Club, it started," she said. "He invited me to see his garden, which I thought was great because I needed pictures to go with the article. Honestly, despite what a nut he was, his garden really was spectacular.

"I toured a few of the other members' gardens so the article wasn't just about Grady, but you wouldn't know it the way he acted. He brought flowers to the newspaper, and at the time, I thought it was just a very nice thank-you, but no. It was just the beginning."

Lindsey glanced at Sully. His expression was

171

grave. It was clear Grady had an MO and he'd used it on both of them.

The waitress returned with their food, and Lindsey waited until she left before she asked, "Then what happened?"

"More flowers, then he started showing up where I got my coffee in the morning," Chloe said. "Then I was on a date, and he was in the restaurant. It was not a coincidence. Then he started emailing me and calling me. Not every day and not all day long, just often enough that it was creepy but if I complained to anyone, they thought I was crazy. He was married. He seemed so nice. Couldn't a guy be nice without a woman making a big deal out of it? Blah, blah, blah."

"Because he never said anything threatening or weird," Lindsey said. "He was just there, a presence, making you feel uncomfortable in your own skin."

"Exactly," Chloe said. She took a bite of her meal, looking as if she was hardly tasting it. "When you read his texts and such, they all seem friendly, but there's an almost imperceptible inappropriateness to them. His smirky smile and the way he just sat there at the restaurant, staring at me while I was on my date, was so unnerving. My date, who was a fix-up, thought I was completely nuts when I made him take me home after the appetizers. That night I got a text from Grady, telling me how pretty I looked."

"That is creepy, but what made you leave town the way you did?" Sully asked. "I mean, you left your job and moved out onto an island. That's pretty drastic."

"I know," Chloe said. She took a sip of the beer she had ordered. Lindsey noticed she was relaxing a bit. Maybe it was because Grady was dead, or perhaps it was because she realized she wasn't alone in this. "There's no way to explain how vulnerable that guy made me feel. He was literally always there, watching me. No matter where I went or what I did, I felt like he was there all the time. Once, when I went home, I was certain someone had been in my house. Things were sort of in the same place I had left them but just a little off, you know?"

Lindsey shivered. She had never even considered this possibility. What if he had tried to get into their house when Heathcliff was there alone? Would he have hurt her dog? The mere thought made Lindsey's heart spasm in her chest.

"After my first article came out in the *New Haven Register*, I got this weird text from a number I didn't recognize with detailed wedding plans. Something like June first would be a great day to get married, and I would of course carry a bouquet of roses from his garden. It went on and on, describing my dress, the food, the color of the roses that would be woven in my hair. I completely freaked out."

Lindsey remembered getting the creepy text when she was trying on wedding dresses. "I can imagine."

"I showed the text to the local police, but there was no way to tell who it was from, and they didn't see anything threatening in it," Chloe said. "One officer actually thought it was just a spam text from a store or something. No one would take me seriously, and I had this feeling I was going to end up kidnapped and living below ground in a root cellar, wearing a wedding dress and having roses in my hair for the rest of my life, which I was beginning to think was going to be cut unduly short."

Her brown eyes were wide, and it was clear that Grady had scared Chloe to death.

"Did you tell your family?" Sully asked.

"No, I'm from Kentucky, and my family would have thought this was a great reason for me to pack up my zany idea of being a journalist and come home, marry Kevin Thompson, my high school sweetheart who manages the car dealership in town, and settle down, maybe be a teacher if I felt the need to do something more than homemaking."

"Oh," Lindsey said.

Chloe smiled. "Yeah, I see myself as more of a Christiane Amanpour. My family, not so much."

"How did you end up out on the Thumb Islands?" Sully asked.

"My roommate at Boston University hooked me up," she said. "Her family has a place on Gull Island. They're renting a villa in Tuscany for the season, so no one was going to be on the island all summer. Her mom thought it was a shame and asked if I'd like to spend the summer out there, taking care of the place. I jumped on it, figuring I could do my writing from there, and other than a few grocery runs, I haven't left the island in weeks."

"Do you think Grady followed you here?" Lindsey asked.

"I don't believe in coincidences," Chloe said.

"Me neither," Lindsey agreed.

They stared at each other, knowing that no one else could appreciate what they'd experienced while being the obsession of Aaron Grady.

"How do you feel about telling the chief of police what you've told us?" Sully asked. "If this is a pattern, and it looks like it is, there could be other women out there that Grady has stalked."

"Which means there might be other people who wanted him dead," Lindsey said. She glanced between Sully and Chloe. "Right now all three of us are people of interest. We need to know if there is anyone else who had a more compelling reason to kill him."

Chloe nodded. "I think you're right. I think there are more women out there. It doesn't make sense that it's just the two of us. I'll talk to the police."

"Thank you," Lindsey said. "I think that's a good call."

"Me, too," Sully said.

They finished their meal, talking about the area and giving Chloe tips on things to do and see for the rest of the summer. She seemed like a nice woman, and Lindsey felt bad that they had met under such horrible circumstances.

"Are you a reader?" Lindsey asked.

"Mostly nonfiction," Chloe said. "I love memoirs, especially of strong women."

"Who are your favorites?"

"Eleanor Roosevelt," Chloe said. "Talk about a woman who didn't suffer fools. Also Madeleine Albright and, more sentimentally, Princess Diana."

"The library has a fabulous collection of female biographies," Lindsey said. "I'm just saying."

Chloe laughed, and it was a delightfully robust sound. "Now that I feel safe to leave the island, I'll be sure to pop in."

Sully paid the bill before Lindsey could grab it. She gave him a look and he shrugged. She'd have to be quicker next time. They all headed for the door. Robbie was still at the bar, and Lindsey waved for him to follow them. She wanted to introduce him to Chloe so that she felt as if she had friends in town. While living on the island seemed idyllic, at some point it had to get lonely.

It was dark when they left the Blue Anchor, but the air was still and the evening felt just as hot and sticky as the day had been. They were halfway across the parking lot when she saw Emma coming their way, and she wasn't alone. Sandwiched between Emma and Detective Trimble from the state police was Sylvia Grady. Lindsey felt her stomach flip-flop like a fish on land. She knew seconds before Sylvia saw them that this was going to be unpleasant.

Sylvia glanced at them and then stopped walking, as if shock had rooted her to the ground. She took in the sight of them and then pointed at them. In a high-pitched shriek of a voice, she cried, "Murderer!"

11

"O h no," Chloe said. "Not her. Not now."

"You've tangled with Sylvia before?" Lindsey asked.

"She's one of the reasons I moved," Chloe said. "She started telling everyone in town that I was trying to steal her husband. As if I would."

"We had a go-round, too," Lindsey said. "So this should be fun."

Sylvia broke away from Emma and the detective and charged them. Her round face was red and sweaty, and her glasses slid to the end of her nose. She pushed them up with a stubby finger as she stomped toward them.

"You!" She pointed at Chloe and then rounded on Lindsey. "And you! I should have known! The two of you are in cahoots. How long have you been planning his murder? How long?"

Sylvia was dressed in business attire consisting of a gray skirt with a matching blazer over a white blouse. A pin was stuck in her lapel, the kind given out for employees who'd lasted ten years or more. This one had a medical emblem over a rising sun, so maybe she was a nurse. The thought horrified Lindsey.

Sylvia didn't wait for an answer to her question but instead launched herself at Chloe.

"What the hell?" Emma cried. She jumped forward to grab Sylvia, but she wasn't quick enough.

Sylvia grabbed a hank of Chloe's hair and yanked the young woman toward her. Lindsey and Sully both jumped forward to protect Chloe. Lindsey caught Sylvia's hand and used the bend-the-index-finger-back technique that Emma had taught them in their one-time self-defense class. With a yelp, Sylvia let go.

"Oy, why do I always miss the good stuff?" Robbie dashed out of the restaurant behind them.

Detective Trimble grabbed Sylvia around the middle and hauled her back a few paces. She was huffing and puffing and trying to jerk out of his hold. Emma moved to stand right in front of her. She glowered and snapped, "Stop it, or I'll use my Taser on you. Don't think I won't."

Sylvia immediately began to sob and wail. Trimble jerked his head in the direction of the station. "I'll take her back. You find out what this is about, and bring food with you when you come back."

"Right," Emma said. She turned toward Lindsey and Chloe, who was rubbing the sore spot on her head. Emma looked equal parts furious and interested. "Explain."

"We were actually on our way to see you,"

Lindsey said. At Emma's doubtful expression, she added, "I swear."

"Come on," Sully said. "Let's go talk in my office, where it's quiet." He jerked his head in the direction of the gawkers who had gathered at the restaurant windows.

Emma gave them a brusque nod and began to walk down the pier. Robbie fell into step beside her, and she arched an eyebrow at him. "What do you have to do with this?"

"Me?" He put a hand on his chest in a protestation of innocence. "I can't imagine what you mean."

"Uh-huh."

Sully's office had been locked up for the night. He used his key to open the door, and they all entered. There were two couches in the corner. Lindsey and Chloe took one; Robbie and Emma took the other. Sully wheeled Ronnie's desk chair out and sat in it, facing the group.

"Emma Plewicki, this is Chloe Weber," Lindsey said. "Chloe, Emma is the Briar Creek chief of police."

"Oh," Chloe said. Then her eyes went wide as it registered. "Oh!"

Emma studied her and said, "Care to share why Sylvia called you a murderer and tried to rip the hair off your head?"

Chloe's shoulders sank, and Lindsey reached over and patted her back. "Hey, remember, you're not alone. Just tell Emma what you told us."

Chloe glanced at Lindsey and then swallowed hard and lifted her head to meet Emma's hard stare. "I wrote an article about Aaron Grady's rose garden last year. Afterward, he began stalking me, and I had to pack up and move. I even changed my name to get away from him."

Emma's eyebrows lifted. Her posture relaxed and she said, "Go on."

Chloe told Emma exactly what she'd told Lindsey and Sully. When she was finished, Emma had her chin cupped in her hand, and she was tapping her jaw with her index finger, as if pondering all this information.

"I'll need you to come to the station and make a formal statement," she said.

"All right," Chloe said. "And just so you know, I didn't kill Grady. I didn't even know he was dead until Lindsey called me."

Emma's head turned in Lindsey's direction. "About that. How did you find Chloe?"

Lindsey recounted the phone calls she'd made. She left Robbie out of it, but Emma wasn't fooled. She glanced at him and said, "You knew about this, didn't you?"

"Only in a passing sort of way," he said.

"Right," she said. She turned back to Chloe. "Aaron Grady was murdered early this morning; can you account for your whereabouts at that time?"

Chloe's face went pale. She looked at Lindsey, her eyes wide with worry. Then she shook her head.

"No, I live alone," she said. "I haven't been off my island in over a week. I only came in today to meet Lindsey."

"Has anyone been out to your island?" Emma asked.

"No," Chloe said. "I'm house-sitting for a family who is traveling."

Emma nodded. "If you can think of any way to confirm your whereabouts, that would be great."

"Am I going to be arrested?" Chloe asked.

"Not at this time," Emma said. Her voice was soft. "But you are a person of interest, so I suggest you not leave the area until further notice."

Chloe looked stricken. Lindsey nudged her with an elbow. "Don't worry." She gestured between herself and Sully. "We're also persons of interest, so it's like a club."

"A really bad club no one wants to be in," Sully said. Then he smiled. "So welcome."

Chloe chuckled, and Lindsey was hit with how much she appreciated Sully's ability to try to cheer up others. It was a good quality to have in a husband. He was going to be her husband. Sometimes—at the weirdest times, in fact—the reality just sneaked up on her that they were getting married and soon. The thought filled her with joy, which was immediately tempered by the realization that they'd better figure out who killed Aaron Grady, so that Sully wouldn't be arrested for a crime he didn't commit.

"Do you know when we'll get a ballistics report back?" Lindsey asked.

"Trimble asked them to rush it, but you know the crime lab," Emma said.

"They'll get to it when they can," Lindsey said.

"Exactly," Emma said. She rose from her seat. She took her phone out and called a number. "Hey, I'm taking Chloe Weber to the station for her statement. Could you keep Mrs. Grady away from the lobby?" There was a pause. "Thanks."

Emma hung up the phone and glanced at Chloe. "You ready?"

Chloe nodded. She rose to her feet, and Lindsey was pleased to see that her spine was stiff and she wasn't looking as timid as she had when she first arrived. They all walked outside.

"Chloe, I can give you a ride back to your island when you're done at the station," Sully said. "It's tricky to navigate the water out there in the dark."

"Thanks, but don't worry about me," Chloe said. "I'm the daughter of a former navy man. He'd have considered it a dereliction of his fatherly duty not to teach his kids how to navigate all sorts of boats, day or night, in all types of water."

To their credit, no one batted an eye at her admission. Lindsey and Sully watched Chloe walk between Emma and Robbie down the pier toward the station, and for just the briefest moment, Lindsey wondered, if Chloe's dad was a navy man, could she have gotten his gun? Might she be the killer after all?

"You're awfully quiet," Sully said. "Are you all right?"

They were home, sitting outside on the back deck while Heathcliff ran around the yard, smelling all the smells. He was in his glory now that his people were home for the night. Lindsey watched him track the scents as he tried to figure out who had been in his yard. He reminded her of a detective searching for clues.

Lindsey glanced at Sully. The air was still hot and heavy. Moths flittered in and out of the yellow porch light. Over the rise that separated their yard from the beach, Lindsey could hear the waves crashing, and the faintest breeze, little more than a puff of breath, moved the air across her skin.

"I'm just turning over the possibility that Chloe is the person who shot Grady," she said. "I don't want to believe it, but if she packed up everything and moved and then the person she was trying to get away from showed up in her new home, well, she might have snapped."

"And her father is former navy," Sully said. "So it's possible she had access to a service revolver like the SIG Sauer."

"Exactly," Lindsey said.

"Except that doesn't answer the question of where my gun went," Sully said. "Chloe couldn't have taken it. She didn't know me or you or any of us before today. And I just have a hinky feeling that the weapon used to kill Grady was mine."

"Really?" Lindsey asked. "Did Emma show you the weapon that was recovered at the scene? Could you identify it if it was yours?"

"No, it was already bagged and tagged and off to the crime lab by the time I caught up to the situation," Sully said.

"Any word from Ian or Charlie about the security video?"

"Charlie is downloading it tonight," he said. "Emma requested all the footage we have, but most of it's stored on the cloud, so Charlie is duplicating it while he downloads it for Emma so we can review it, too. The problem is we only keep a month's worth of video. If someone broke in and took my gun before that, we'll have no record of it."

"Who knew you kept your gun there?" she asked.

"Just Ronnie, Ian and me. We're the only ones with access to the safe."

"So it makes no sense that Chloe would have

broken into your office and stolen your gun to shoot Grady," Lindsey said.

"No, I've never even met her before today," he said. "And I believe her when she says she didn't know Grady was here in town. I don't think you can fake that sort of shock."

"You really think your gun was the weapon used to kill Grady?"

Sully met her gaze, and his look was concerned. "Yes, which means whoever did it knew that Grady and I had words at the restaurant, and they were looking to set me up for the murder."

"Then it seems that the most likely time of the break-in was last night after our incident at the Blue Anchor but before Robbie and I found the body," she said.

"And I'm hoping the video shows it," Sully said.

A yawn slipped out of Lindsey, and she relaxed back in her chair. The horrendous events of the day had finally caught up with her, and she could feel sleep claiming her for the night.

"Come on," Sully said. "Let's call it a day. We can talk more about this tomorrow. With any luck, Charlie will have found something on the video."

They rolled out of the chairs, and Lindsey whistled for Heathcliff to come. He bounded up the steps and onto the deck. Lindsey bent down and rubbed his ears. He was such a fierce protector of his people. She remembered the night he had growled at Grady when he had arrived here uninvited. It was a relief to Lindsey that she no longer had to look over her shoulder, but there was no way she'd let Grady's murder get pinned on Sully.

There had to be a way to find out who had wanted Grady dead and who had wanted it badly enough to do it.

12

Charlie called early in the morning and asked Sully to meet him at the office. He had downloaded all the security videos and was in the process of cleaning them up so the resolution was better.

Lindsey offered to go, too, but Sully told her to go ahead and meet her parents for breakfast and that he'd call her if they found anything. She watched him go, hoping they would. A nice close-up of a person stealing Sully's gun would go a long way to boosting her morale.

She enjoyed omelets with her folks, careful not to let anything slip about Grady or the gun or Sully being a suspect. Thankfully, their visit with the Sullivans had been busy and gave them plenty to talk about, and they didn't notice that Lindsey was quieter than usual. Afterward, she took Heathcliff for a run on the beach. Sometimes a gal just had to try to outrun her demons, and as Lindsey pounded down the sandy shore, she hoped she was leaving some of hers behind.

The day was already hot, and she lingered under the cold spray of the shower, knowing full well that as soon as she got out, she'd be hot and wet, making the whole process of showering rather pointless.

She dressed for work, planning to head over to the dock to see whether any progress had been made, then heard a car pull into her driveway. She glanced outside and recognized Emma. She wondered whether she was here to see Sully. Curious, Lindsey stepped out the front door with Heathcliff at her side.

"Good morning, Em," she called. "Can I get you some coffee?"

"Always," Emma said. She trudged up the stairs and followed Lindsey into the house. "Is Sully here?"

"No, he already left for work," Lindsey said. "Do you need him?"

She watched Emma's face, looking for an indication of why she wanted Sully. Was she going to arrest him?

"Actually, it was you I wanted to see," Emma said. She took the cup of coffee Lindsey poured. She drank it black, which Lindsey admired. She supposed years of no sleep and staying up late had given Emma the fortitude to down the bitter brew, but Lindsey was a dribble-of-milk-and-spoonful-of-sugar type of coffee drinker, and she didn't think that would change anytime soon.

"What about?" Lindsey asked.

Emma studied her for a moment. She blew out a breath and said, "Do you have some time this morning? I want to show you something."

Her tone was serious, alarmingly so. Lindsey resisted the urge to crack wise to lessen the tension. Whatever was making the pinched lines around Emma's eyes was not something to joke about.

"I don't have to go in until later this morning since I'm closing tonight," Lindsey said. "I'm free now."

"Good," Emma said. Lindsey got the feeling she'd already known this, and she wasn't sure how she felt about that. "Let's go."

"Where?"

"You'll see."

They rode in the squad car. Lindsey sat in front even though there was hardly any room around all the gadgetry mounted to Emma's dashboard. They moved at a quick clip through town, not officially speeding but definitely going a few miles faster than was posted. Lindsey supposed she should be grateful that Emma hadn't fired up the sirens on her charge through town.

They left the center of Briar Creek behind, and the road opened up to a stretch of large homes with scrupulously maintained lawns—or they would have been if it were not for the drought. The grass was dry and yellow, looking brittle and scorched. Yard after yard had the same haggard appearance. Not even in this affluent area could the residents fight off the effects of the longest dry spell to have hit the area in years. It was into one of these driveways that Emma turned.

The house was a single-story redbrick house that sprawled in several directions. An enormous picture window overlooked a large fountain in the center of the front yard. Spiraling out from the fountain in a profusion of brilliant colors were roses of every color and hue imaginable.

"Oh no," Lindsey said. She looked at Emma. "Really? Why?"

"There's something you need to see."

Well, didn't that sound ominous? Lindsey followed Emma as she climbed out of the car and began to stride across the grounds. Lindsey glanced at the house, wondering whether Sylvia was here. And if she was, was she going to come flying out of the house in another tirade? Lindsey didn't know if she was up for that this early in the morning.

"She's not here," Emma said. She was watching Lindsey as if trying to gauge how she reacted to that news.

"Oh, good," Lindsey said. "I mean, it'd be weird to be here with her here. Not that I have a problem with her being here—oh God, I'm going to stop talking now."

"Probably for the best," Emma said.

She led Lindsey around the side of the house to the backyard. There were even more roses here, and the smell under the heat of the hot day was almost overpowering. She felt as if she were breathing in spun sugar. It made her throat close up, and she took a slow breath in, trying to open up the passageway.

"You all right?" Emma asked. She looked concerned, and Lindsey was relieved to see the cop facade crack and to find her friend in there.

"Yeah, just not really a fan of roses," Lindsey said.

Emma looked as if she understood. "Let's try to be quick, then, and get you out of here."

She led Lindsey toward the far corner of the yard, where there was an old, weathered gardening shed. It had double doors, one of which was open, and inside Lindsey saw the familiar uniform of the state crime scene personnel. She glanced at Emma in alarm.

"There isn't a body in there, is there?" she asked. "Because I've really had my fill lately."

"No, I promise." Emma stepped into the shed and gestured for the crime scene guy to step aside. "Sorry, Ted, we'll be out of your way in a second."

"No problem," Ted said. He was middle-aged with a mustache and glasses, and he was holding a camera in front of him as if it were a shield. He moved back a few paces to give them some room.

There were numbered yellow markers all over the shed, indicating areas of interest. Clearly, the police had found something in the shed that was connected to the murder of Aaron Grady.

Lindsey glanced around the small space. There were rakes and shovels hanging from a pegboard on the wall, bottles of herbicide and pesticide, and several bags of potting soil sorted on a low shelf. A stack of pots and a box of assorted seeds were on a workbench. On the floor there was a roughly cut section of carpet that looked to be brand new, and it was rolled back to reveal a dark stain on the exposed plank flooring.

It was then that Lindsey noticed the faint smell of bleach, as if someone had been doing some cleaning out here. She glanced at Emma in confusion.

"Was this where Aaron Grady was killed?" she asked.

"Possibly," Emma said. "What I wanted you to see is over here."

There was a wide metal cabinet in the corner. A broken combination lock hung off one of its handles. The double doors were ajar but not open. Emma pulled on a blue latex glove that Ted handed her and gently opened the cabinet.

On the inside of the door on the right was a collage. It was all pictures and paper mementos of Lindsey. She blinked. There was the scratch piece of paper on which she'd written the call number for roses. There were close-up photos of her face, one in which she was frowning at a book she was reading and one in which she was laughing. There were pictures of her biking through town and a bookmark that she used while at the reference desk that she'd thought she'd misplaced. There was a large photo of her in a bridal gown from the day she'd gone gown shopping. It looked as if it had been taken through the shop window. Thankfully, it was not the dress she had chosen to buy. That would have ruined it, but still, it was unsettling. Draped across it all was a long strand of blond hair that was definitely hers.

Lindsey took a step back. She felt a bit woozy. She put her fingers over her mouth, but she wasn't sure whether she was trying to prevent herself from hyperventilating or keeping a scream in. Grady had been creepy, but this brought home to her just how unhinged the man had been, and even though he was dead, for the first time, she felt very, very afraid of what he might have done, of what could have happened. She stumbled out of the shed, needing to get some air.

"Just give me a second," she said. Outside, she bent over, trying to calm her racing heart and get some oxygen into her lungs. The stifling scent of the roses wasn't making her feel any better.

Emma followed her out. She leaned over beside Lindsey and dabbed something under her nose. Lindsey reared back at the sharp smell.

"What is that?"

"Mentholated ointment," Emma said. "We used

it at the police academy when we had to sit in on autopsies. It cuts the smell of just about anything, including roses." She showed Lindsey the tiny tube in her hand. "I always carry a bit with me, because you never know when you're going to need it."

Lindsey took a deep breath through her nose. It helped. She could feel the dizziness dissipate, and she met the police chief's gaze. "Thanks."

"Can you go back in there?" Emma asked. "I wanted to ask you about some of the specifics."

"Yeah," Lindsey said. She hoped she sounded more confident than she felt.

Ted passed them on their way in. He looked at Lindsey with sympathy and then said, "I've got all the photos I need. I'm going to start bagging it for the lab."

"Just give us a few minutes," Emma said.

"Take your time," he said. He walked off to where the van was parked, and Lindsey noticed there were other crime scene people in the house. She wondered how Sylvia was dealing with all of this.

"You ready?" Emma asked.

"Yeah," Lindsey said.

They moved to stand in front of the cabinet. This time Lindsey was prepared. Emma asked her about each photograph, and Lindsey did her best to try to remember where and when they could have been taken. Emma took notes while she talked. When they were finished, Lindsey glanced at the other door. Not surprisingly, it was a shrine similar to hers, but it was made up of photos of Chloe Weber.

Lindsey looked at the rest of the cabinet. There were no other photos or mementos. She found that odd. She had assumed Grady had stalked more than just the two of them. She glanced at the shelves in the cabinet. There were more tools, some paint, hose fixtures and a watering pitcher. Most of the shelves were dusty or had smears of dirt, all except for the middle one. That one was clean. Lindsey bent down so that she was crouched on the floor.

"Are you all right?" Emma asked.

"Don't you find it odd that this shelf isn't as dirty as the others?" Lindsey asked. It was too dark to see in the small space. She glanced up at Emma. "Can I borrow your flashlight?"

Emma crouched down beside her and handed her a small penlight. Lindsey shone it on the underside of the shelf. Staring down at them was an image of a woman dressed in a wedding gown with a small smile on her face. She was pretty with big blue eyes and long blond hair.

Lindsey didn't know who she was, but she knew who she wasn't. "That's not Sylvia."

"No, it isn't." Emma frowned. "Don't touch it. I'm going to call for Ted."

Emma stepped into the doorway to call back

the crime scene technician. While she had her back turned, Lindsey took a moment to snap a picture of the photo with her phone. Emma hadn't said not to, and she wanted to study it more closely and see whether she could figure out who this woman was and what she must have meant to Grady. She had delicate features and a cute upturned nose; she seemed young.

As soon as she had a decent picture, Lindsey straightened up and stepped around Emma to stand outside.

"It's hot in there," she muttered.

Emma nodded. She was waving at Ted, who raised his arm to signal that he was on his way back.

Lindsey hadn't been exaggerating. The tiny shed had been oppressive, and she felt as if she couldn't breathe. The sun was hot, so she took shelter in a small patch of shade to the side of the shed. She wondered about the pretty woman in the photo. Had she been an obsession of Grady's, too? It seemed likely.

Lindsey studied the picture on her phone and tried to determine the age of the photo by the style of the wedding gown. It was definitely older, with enormous puffy sleeves and a lacy top; the woman's hair was a big permed mass of curls; and there was an explosion of tulle on the back of her head. Lindsey could tell it was a few decades old at least, but Beth was the wedding expert. She'd be able to pinpoint the year on this, for sure. Lindsey shielded her phone from the glare of daylight to see better. She could tell the photo, which was in color, had begun to fade, another indicator of its age.

She saw Ted coming back, and she slid her phone into her pocket. Emma gave Ted instructions as he joined her in the shed. Lindsey waited. She heard Ted give an exclamation of surprise. In moments, Emma came out to join her, and she said, "Come on—I'll take you back to town."

"Thanks," Lindsey said. She knew from checking her phone that it was time for her to get to work. "You can just drop me off at the library."

They were quiet as they drove. Lindsey had a million questions, but she had no idea how to ask them without making a nuisance of herself. Contrary to what the chief of police probably believed, Lindsey didn't mean to be a bother. It was Emma who finally broke the silence when she parked in front of the library and waited while Lindsey gathered her things.

"Lindsey, there's something I forgot to ask you, and I wanted to clarify it now, if that's all right."

"Okay." Lindsey met Emma's gaze.

"Did you know that Sully kept his gun locked up in his office?"

"Yes, I did," she said. She tried to read Emma's face. Was she just gathering facts, or was there a more specific reason she needed this bit of information? Emma gave her nothing.

"Okay, thanks," Emma said. She didn't even flicker an eyelash.

Lindsey slid out of the car. She shut the door behind her and watched Emma drive away, realizing she had just made herself a probable suspect in the murder of Aaron Grady.

13

Lindsey tried to act as though it were business as usual for the rest of the morning, but she was off her game, as evidenced by the fact that she found herself trying to log on to her cell phone as if it were her computer. She had called Sully after her field trip with Emma, and he had said he'd stop by the library around lunchtime. Lindsey tried not to watch the clock. Tried and failed.

Telling Emma that she knew where Sully's gun was kept felt like an admission of guilt, which was crazy because she knew she hadn't done anything wrong. But there was no doubt that the pictures of her in Grady's shed made it look as if she had a pretty big motive to rub out the guy, who was clearly obsessed.

She wondered whether Emma had brought Chloe to look at the pictures as well. Did Chloe look like more of a suspect than Lindsey or Sully? She felt terrible for hoping that the woman did, but she absolutely did.

Then, of course, there was the lone photo on the underside of the shelf. Who was that woman? With Grady dead, was there any way to find out?

Would Sylvia know her? The picture had been old, but it was still in the cabinet with the others. It had to have meant something to Grady.

Lindsey shook her head. The whole thing made her feel sordid, as if she was contaminated by his malevolence just by association. Chloe had said he was obsessed with marrying her and that he'd been sending her plans for their wedding. That fell in line with his stalking Lindsey while she was buying a wedding dress, but he was already married, so what was his interest in the two of them? Did he believe in having more than one wife?

She shivered. She wondered whether there would be even more grisly discoveries at the Grady home, and she wasn't sure she wanted to know.

"Hey, darlin', got a minute?" Sully appeared in the doorway, looking pale and tired. The fine lines around his eyes looked deeper, and he looked like a man who needed a cup of coffee about as desperately as he needed air to breathe.

"For you? Always," she said.

"Aw, that's sweet." Ian popped up behind Sully. "You should marry that girl."

Ian was short and bald, bespectacled and freckled, but his personality was the friendliest Lindsey had ever encountered. He truly believed a stranger was just a friend he hadn't met yet, and he could charm even the crankiest person into a laugh or a grin. It was no mystery to Lindsey why Mary, his wife, was completely smitten with him.

"You're right," Sully said. "I think I will."

Lindsey laughed at the pair of them, and realized it was the first time she'd smiled all day.

"What are you two up to?" she asked. She knew Ian wouldn't be here if it wasn't important, as he should be prepping for the dinner rush at the Blue Anchor.

"We just dropped off the security videos with Emma at the police department," Sully said.

"But we also made a copy for ourselves just in case we need it," Ian said. "You can't be too careful in a case like this."

Lindsey thought about the picture she'd taken of the mystery woman. "Agreed."

Sully met her gaze. "When we were at the station, we saw some of the pictures from Grady's shed. Are you all right?"

Lindsey shrugged. "I will be."

"Especially when they catch whoever did this," Ian said. "Speaking of which, we have something to show you." He pulled a thumb drive out of his pocket. He gestured to her computer, and Lindsey waved him in.

"Go for it," she said. While Ian set it up, she turned to Sully and asked, "Did you see anything significant?"

"I'm going to leave it to you to decide," he said.

"All right, we're ready." Ian opened the drive and then the file they wanted her to see.

It took the computer a moment to read the file, but then a video filled the screen. It was grainy, but Lindsey could make out the exterior of Sully's office. As she watched, the front door opened, and Ronnie, recognizable by her big hairdo, and a man Lindsey didn't know walked out of the office. They moved to the edge of the pier and were deep in conversation when another person walked down the pier toward the shop. The person paused. Then resumed walking. Lindsey gasped. She recognized the way the man kept his head at an odd angle while he walked. It was Aaron Grady.

Both Sully and Ian turned to ask her what she'd seen, but Lindsey held up her hand. She wanted to keep watching. She wanted to be sure.

Grady slipped into the office without Ronnie noticing. He was in the building for mere minutes, and then he was back out and walking down the pier toward town. Ronnie and her companion never noticed him.

"When was this?" Lindsey asked.

"Three days ago. Just before the shooting. Do you recognize the man?" Sully asked.

"Yes, it was Aaron Grady. I'm sure of it."

"I knew it!" Ian said. He punched his fist in the air. "That guy was obviously up to something, and it went horribly wrong for him."

"Yes, but what?" Sully asked. "I mean, if it is him and he stole my gun, what was he planning to do? He didn't commit suicide, because according to Emma, he wasn't killed behind the library. He was shot somewhere else, and then his body was moved."

"Which begs another question," Lindsey said. "Who wanted his death tied to the library?"

"Someone who knew about his altercation with you two and wanted to make it look as if you were involved somehow," Ian said.

"Have you told Emma that it's him? That Aaron Grady is the one who stole your gun?" Lindsey asked.

"No, I didn't want to taint the video for her, and I can't prove he took the gun," Sully said. "It shows him going into the office, which we know is empty, but it's not like we see him going into the safe and taking the weapon."

"But he did," Lindsey said. "I know it." She glanced at Sully, aware of Ian watching them. "What do you think he was going to do with the gun?"

"No idea," Sully said. He said it quickly, practically tripping over the words to get them out. Lindsey knew he was thinking the same thing she was, but he didn't want to say it.

"I think he was either going to shoot me and frame you," she said. "That would have gotten even with both of us, me for not wanting him and you for being in the way. Or he was going to shoot you and probably try to make it look like a suicide, thinking that I would be free to be with him then." She couldn't keep the revulsion out of her voice.

Sully reached for her. He hugged her tight, burying his face in her hair and resting his chin in the curve between her neck and her shoulder. She wasn't sure who was comforting whom, but she'd take it any way she could get it. The thought that either of them might have died at Grady's hand was too horrible to contemplate.

"Well, I can see you two have things in order here," Ian said. He cleared his throat and headed for the door. "I'll just shuffle back to the restaurant, hug my wife and daughter and, you know, never let them out of my sight ever again, not even to go to the bathroom."

Sully lifted his head with a laugh. "Mary will clobber you if you even suggest it."

"I might not tell her," Ian said. He winked at them both and then sobered. "I'm glad you two are all right, but be careful. We don't know who shot Grady or why, and the nightmare may not be over yet."

"We will," Lindsey said.

They watched him leave, and she studied Sully and said, "We need to figure out who the third woman is. She could be our killer."

"Agreed," he said. "So what's the plan?"

"I'm not sure," Lindsey said. "I think we need to find out everything we can about Aaron Grady—you know, like where he was born and raised, where he went to school, does he have any family? We need to find someone who could tell us about him, someone other than his wife. I want to talk to Chloe and see what she learned about his backstory for her article. Maybe it will point us in the right direction."

"Unless she's the killer, in which case it might get us dead," he said.

"True," Lindsey said. "We'll need to bring some backup."

"When you said 'backup,' this was not what I had in mind," Sully said. They were cruising amid the islands in his water taxi, headed for Gull Island.

Lindsey was in the seat beside him, and she looked over her shoulder to see Robbie and Charlie sharing the bench seat in back. The two were at odds, with Robbie's fair-haired movie-star good looks and Charlie's rough-and-tumble, messy long black hair that he currently had twisted into a man bun on the top of his head. It was the first time Lindsey had ever gotten a good look at his face, as it was usually covered by a curtain of long, stringy rock-star hair. She realized Charlie was actually quite good looking, in a sweaty boy-band kind of way. The man bun, however, was best ignored. She figured it was the mullet of their age and hopefully would pass into obscurity like duck lips any day now.

She glanced back at Sully and shrugged. "They were available."

It was late afternoon, and the sun was still high in the sky, baking them with its blistering heat but not burning off the oppressive humidity that lingered in the air. Thankfully, the speed of the boat made enough of a breeze to cool Lindsey's skin.

"How do you know which house Chloe is staying in on the island?" Lindsey asked.

"My parents are good friends with the Carstairs, who are spending the summer in Tuscany. I figured it has to be them, especially given that their daughter went to Boston University and is about the same age as Chloe," he said. "It all fit."

"Nice detective work," she said.

Sully smiled. "Thanks, I learned how from this librarian I know."

Lindsey laughed. Oh, he was a charmer, her future husband. Her amusement faded quickly, however, as she recalled that their entire future as a married couple was precariously balanced on the evidence tied to Grady's murder.

If the gun used was Sully's, they were up a creek. And if they couldn't prove that Grady was the one who had stolen the gun from Sully's office, they were without a paddle. If Emma was forced to arrest Sully based on that evidence, then they were swiftly headed for a waterfall.

The mental image made Lindsey's heart constrict in her chest. She forced herself to breathe. There was no reason to panic. Not yet. They still had the picture of the third woman to identify and Grady's past to dig through, both of which could change everything.

Sully cut the engine and glided up to the dock. Their boat bumped alongside the bobbing wooden planks with a gentle nudge, and Charlie hopped out and tied up their boat while Sully secured their belongings. Charlie gave Lindsey a hand to help her climb out, and Robbie followed her. Sully stepped out last, and as a group they headed toward the stairs that scaled a sharp rocky cliff to the island above, where the houses perched overlooking the water.

The Thumb Islands had been a resort location for the very wealthy in the early nineteen hundreds. Much like Newport, Rhode Island, it was a famous spot for wealthy New Yorkers to escape the city back in the day. The original buildings had been primarily Victorians, with arched windows, turrets and wraparound porches. It had been a thriving community. One of the islands had a fancy hotel, another a grocery, and still another had a movie theater and a bowling alley. All of that had changed after the hurricane of 'thirty-eight, when the wind and rain had wiped clean most of the islands, dumping the towering Victorians into the bay.

Since then, the houses were mostly summer cottages. The buildings now were a mixed bag of utilitarian and ostentatious, from islands that were essentially big rocks with one cottage to large hilly multi-acre islands that sported several mansions with all the amenities. Gull Island, like Bell Island, where Sully's parents lived, was one of the larger and more civilized islands.

The Carstairs' house was a modern building, one of the few in the archipelago, and it was a nod to midcentury modern design, made primarily of concrete and steel, with loads of angles and floor-to-ceiling windows offering breathtaking views of the bay. Lindsey didn't often get house envy, but for this one, she definitely felt a twinge.

"Rather posh, isn't it?" Robbie asked as they reached the upper deck and took in the house before them.

"Posh? Does that mean *awesome?*" Charlie asked. "Because it totally is."

"Yes, it does," Lindsey said. "And it sure is."

Lindsey wondered whether Chloe was home. She glanced down at the dock and noted that there were two boats in addition to their own. There were other houses on this island, so it was hard to tell whether the boats were Chloe's or someone else's, since it was a communal dock.

A path led from the upper deck toward the

center of the island. It was lined with red cedar shavings, and they trudged along the path, which turned into a big circle. Individual paths led to each of the houses. It appeared the houses had all been built around the same time, as they were all modern looking, with the same squared-off, concrete-and-steel look.

"How do we know which one belongs to the Carstairs?" Lindsey asked.

"My mom said it's the one closest to the dock," Sully said.

He took the shortest route from the circle to the path that led to the house they'd seen from the dock below. Narrow patches of trees separated each house, giving the residents a bit of privacy. Lindsey wondered what would happen if two residents took a dislike to each other. There really was no way to escape a nosy neighbor out here.

They approached the front door. Lindsey glanced at her companions. Chloe had met Sully and Robbie before, but she hadn't met Charlie. Maybe the man bun was a good thing. It made him seem less threatening.

Lindsey took the lead since she and Chloe had formed a rapport over being the victims of Grady's interest. She looked for a doorbell but couldn't find one, so she settled for knocking on the wooden frame, since the door was made mostly of frosted glass. She stepped back while they waited. No one answered. She glanced at

Sully, who nodded, before she knocked again. Still there was no answer.

"Do we know what her boat looks like?" Charlie asked. "Was it one of the ones tied up at the dock?"

"I don't know. I've never seen her come in or go out, and I have no idea which slip at the marina belongs to the Carstairs," Sully said.

"So she might not be here," Robbie said.

"But there were two boats down there," Lindsey said. "Somebody has to be on the island."

She glanced at the other houses. Neither of them showed any signs of life. She tried the door handle. It wasn't locked. She looked at the group.

"Should we go in?" she asked. "She might be armed and could shoot at us."

"That would be a 'no' vote from me," Robbie said.

"Ditto," Charlie echoed.

"I'll go in," Sully said.

"I'm coming with you," Lindsey said.

He looked as if he wanted to argue, but Lindsey lifted her eyebrows and he wisely thought better of it. "Stay behind me."

"Okay," she said. She turned to Charlie and Robbie. "Can one of you watch the door and the other the boats? If anyone tries to run, I want someone to see them."

"I'll take the boats," Charlie said.

"Door," Robbie said.

They left and Sully and Lindsey turned back to the house. Sully pushed the door open, and they stepped inside. Lindsey wasn't sure whether to call out a greeting or not. Sully glanced at her and put a finger to his lips. He cocked his head, listening. Clearly they were going for the stealth entry.

The door opened up into a foyer. There was a small table with a vase of dried flowers to the right, and the air smelled nicely of lavender and vanilla. As they moved out of the entrance and into the open layout of the house, Lindsey noticed the colors were warm shades of rich brown and pale green. They moved carefully across the dark wooden floor as if expecting it to creak.

Sully paused by the staircase to their right. He glanced over the railing at the kitchen, small dining nook and large living room. There was no one there. Lindsey pulled him close and whispered in his ear, "I'm going to call out a hello. Maybe she was just upstairs and didn't hear us knock."

"Sounds good," he whispered back. He pulled them into the shadows by the wall and nodded.

Lindsey cleared her throat. "Hello? Chloe? It's Lindsey and Sully. We were just in the area and wanted to see how you're doing."

"In the area? Really?" Sully asked, keeping his voice quiet.

Lindsey waved at him to shush. She strained to hear whether there was a response. There was, but it wasn't Chloe answering them.

She heard a thump and a crash and the sound of footsteps pounding down the hallway, headed in their direction. A door slammed into a wall, and Chloe screamed, "Look out! He has a gun!"

14

Sully tucked himself over Lindsey and hauled her to the ground. Someone ran down the steps, but instead of going past them and out the front door, they went into the living room. A door banged open, and then it was quiet. Sully and Lindsey popped their heads up.

"Charlie is out there watching the boats," she said.

"I'm on it."

"Be careful."

"You, too." Sully kissed her quick and then darted across the house, slipping out the door that the person with the gun had just run through. Lindsey thought about going after him but reminded herself that he was ex-navy. He knew what he was doing. She needed to check on Chloe.

She hurried to the stairs and climbed them two at a time. "Chloe? Chloe, are you all right?"

The front door opened when she was halfway up, and she glanced around to see Robbie enter the house.

"Sully sent me in here. Is everything all right?"

"I don't know," Lindsey said. "I haven't found Chloe yet."

There was a thump on the floor in a room above, and Chloe yelled, "Here. I'm in here! Please hurry!"

Lindsey broke into a run with Robbie right on her heels. She darted down the narrow hall, glancing into bedrooms as she passed. When she reached the large master bedroom, she saw Chloe lying on the floor with her hands bound behind her back and her ankles taped together with duct tape. Her long dark hair was spread out across the floor, and she was gasping for breath as a piece of tape hung off the side of her face.

She was struggling to roll up onto her feet. Lindsey darted forward and hefted her up by one arm. Chloe staggered, and Lindsey helped her sit down on the edge of the bed.

"It's okay. We're here," Lindsey said. She snatched the tape off Chloe's face.

"Ouch!" Chloe said.

"Sorry."

Robbie darted into the room, and Chloe started as if she planned to fight him.

"It's okay," Lindsey said. "He's with me."

Robbie was panting and he waved at Chloe. "Hey there. Remember me? I'm dating the police chief. We spent a lovely evening at the station together."

"Oh, yeah." Chloe relaxed. "Sorry."

"Help me get the tape off of her," Lindsey said. She moved to work on the tape on Chloe's wrists while Robbie tried to peel it off her ankles. He fished his keys out of his pocket and gouged a hole in the tape that he then used to rip the tape right off.

Lindsey managed to do the same with the tape on Chloe's wrists, but while her ankles were protected by the socks she was wearing, there was no protection for the skin of her wrists when Lindsey yanked the tape free, probably taking some arm hair with it.

"Ouch!" Chloe cried again.

"Sorry," Lindsey said. She gently pushed Chloe's arms forward, knowing they were probably cramped from being held behind her back for so long. "Are you all right?"

"I'm alive," Chloe said. "I call that a win."

"What happened?" Lindsey asked. "Did you see who attacked you?"

"No, it all happened so fast," Chloe said. "One second I was working on my laptop, and the next I was knocked to the floor. I clunked my head on the way down and must have been knocked out for a bit. I woke up with my hands and feet taped and another strip across my mouth. I managed to work that off by rubbing my face into the carpet."

Lindsey looked at Chloe's face. The skin was red and raw on her cheek and jaw. She must have been terrified.

"I heard you call 'Hello,' and I knew I had to

warn you but also that you were my only hope," Chloe said. A sob bubbled up, and she put her face in her hands and let the tears fall.

Lindsey sat down beside her and put her arm around her. She rubbed her back and said, "It's all right. You're safe. We're here."

Chloe leaned against her, welcoming the comfort. Lindsey glanced over her head at Robbie. He was prowling the room, looking at everything, as if hoping Chloe's attacker had left their business card.

"What do you suppose the attacker wanted?" he asked. "Did it have anything to do with Grady's murder? Or was it a random break-in?"

"It seems unlikely that it was random," Lindsey said.

Chloe raised her head and wiped her face with the palms of her hands. She sniffed and then said, "I heard them tapping on my computer."

"Really?" Robbie said. "Now why would they want to do that?"

Lindsey got up and went over to look at Chloe's laptop, which was on the small desk in front of the window. She glanced through the sheer curtains and noted the spectacular view of the small yard and bay.

Chloe shrugged. "I was writing a piece about child stars and where they are today—"

Robbie let out a huff of breath, and Chloe frowned. "When you're a freelance writer, you write what sells. Besides, I'm actually approaching from the angle of people who walked away from the biz and went on to have really happy lives—you know, like the guy who played Jake Ryan in *Sixteen Candles*. I'm trying to gather current pictures of them all."

Robbie looked chagrined. "I suppose that's a better angle than most."

"Thanks for the approval." Chloe rolled her eyes. "Ouch!" She put her fingers to her right temple. "That hurt."

"You might have a concussion," Lindsey said. She pressed the track pad on Chloe's computer, and the screen lit up. "Robbie, check her eyes and make sure her pupils look normal."

"All right," he said. He bent over so he was level with Chloe. "Open your eyes wide." He studied her for a moment. "They look all right, but she should probably see a doctor. Head injuries are a nasty business."

Lindsey scanned the piece Chloe was working on. The writing was good—short, punchy, irreverent. But then whoever had typed on her laptop had hit return a few times and wrote what looked like a suicide note.

I am filled with guilt for what I've done and the pain I've caused. I wish I could do it over but I can't. I am so very sor—

"Chloe, was your attacker typing when I knocked on the front door?" Lindsey asked.

"Yes, when he . . . she . . . I don't know which," she said.

"Let's go with he for the sake of clarity," Lindsey said. Chloe nodded.

"Okay, when he heard you call hello, he stopped typing. I was trying to roll to the door, but he shoved me down hard and I saw the gun in his hand. I was so scared I kicked at him, but I hit the nightstand and the lamp went over."

"Which is when you warned us that he was armed," Lindsey said.

Chloe looked at Lindsey with a wary expression on her face. "What did he write?"

Lindsey read it to her, and Chloe went pale. "I didn't write that."

"I know," Lindsey said.

"Blimey, that's a suicide note," Robbie said. He looked horrified.

"My attacker was going to kill me and make it look like a suicide," Chloe said. She started to shake.

"Let's get out of here," Lindsey said. "If they left any evidence behind, I don't want to contaminate it."

Chloe looked longingly at her computer, but Lindsey shook her head.

"Fingerprints," she said.

"If we're lucky," Chloe replied. "Ugh, my

computer is my baby. I don't go anywhere without it."

"Can you walk?" Robbie asked. "You're not dizzy or anything?"

"No, I'm okay," Chloe said. "Just a headache."

"Let's go," Lindsey said. "I'm worried about Sully and Charlie."

Robbie held out his arm, and Chloe took it, looking grateful as she rose to her feet with a wince. They made their way out of the master bedroom and back into the hallway. Lindsey scanned the house as they went, on the off chance that whoever had attacked Chloe returned. She tried not to think about what that would mean for Sully or Charlie. She hadn't heard any gunshots, so she assumed they were all right.

Once they were downstairs, Lindsey told Robbie to get a bag of ice for Chloe's head. She wanted to look outside for Sully. Robbie insisted he should do it, but Lindsey ignored him, moving as fast as she could to the side door through which Sully had followed Chloe's assailant. She couldn't shake the feeling that something was wrong.

She hurried outside and saw Charlie crouched by the edge of the yard, right where there was a steep drop to the water below.

"Charlie!" she cried as she ran toward him. "What's going on?"

"It's all right." Charlie huffed. "I've almost got him."

Lindsey broke into a run. She stopped beside him and glanced over the side to see Sully dangling from a shoddy piece of frayed plastic boating rope while Charlie dug in his heels, trying to pull him up.

"Ah!" Lindsey gasped. Sully glanced up at her and grinned.

"I'm all right," he said. He was hanging on to the rope with one hand and clutching a rock with the other. Lindsey felt her heart slam up into her throat. She stepped up beside Charlie and grabbed the rope. They could barely budge it.

"Robbie!" she cried.

In seconds Robbie came running out of the house. He took in the scene at a glance and grabbed the rope, too. Chloe was right behind him, but there was no room to add her to the human chain, and she looked a bit pasty and weak, holding an ice pack to her temple.

"Pull," Robbie ordered. The three of them braced themselves and heaved, using all their strength. Lindsey could feel the strain in every muscle, and she dug deeper, looking for more power, anything to keep Sully from falling. Inch by inch the rope moved until Sully's head popped up over the ledge. Robbie dropped the rope and grabbed Sully's forearm, yanking him up onto the lawn with one mighty heave.

Sully rolled onto the dry lawn as if he was completely out of strength. Lindsey dropped the rope and crawled over to him, hugging him tight. She had never felt so relieved in her life. A glance past him at the drop and she saw the jagged rocks thirty feet below that would have broken him into pieces. She cupped his face and kissed him hard. Then she hit him on the shoulder.

"What happened?" she cried.

"It was my fault," Charlie said. "This guy came flying out of the back of the house. He was dressed all in black with a hoodie pulled tight around his face with sunglasses on. I knew I had to stop him, so I charged at him. But he had a gun so I dropped back, but he still charged me. Sully tackled the guy around the knees, and he dropped the gun. When Sully went to grab it, the guy shoved him, and Sully slipped right over the ledge."

Charlie's eyes were huge, as if he still couldn't believe what he'd seen.

"Thankfully, I was able to grab an outcropping, and then Charlie found some rope, but unfortunately our bad guy got away. I heard a boat motor fire up while I was hanging around," Sully said.

Lindsey gave him a weak smile. He wiped his face with his hand, and she noticed his palms were scraped up and bloody.

"Thanks for coming when you did," Sully said. "I don't think I could have hung on much longer."

He glanced around the grass and then looked at Charlie. "The gun's gone."

Charlie met his gaze and then smiled. "Or is it?" He lifted his shirt and pulled a handgun out of his waistband.

"Charlie, you did it!" Sully cried. He sat up with a grin and slapped Charlie on the back. The gun wobbled in his hands, and they all dropped to the ground.

"Whoa, whoa, whoa, take it easy, cowboy," Robbie said. "Do you know how to use one of those?"

"I've never touched a gun in my life," Charlie said. He looked at it as if it were a live snake. "Take it, please."

Sully held out his hand, and Charlie gently put it in his palm. Sully looked at Lindsey. "Let's call Emma."

"On it," she said. She'd already opened her list of contacts and pressed Emma's number. She held her phone to her ear. Emma picked up on the third ring.

"Lindsey, where is everyone?" she asked. "I can't find Sully or Robbie. Are they with you?"

"Yes," Lindsey said. She then proceeded to tell Emma everything that had happened. At the end of it, Emma was her usual terse self.

"Don't touch anything. Do not move. I'll be right there."

Lindsey glanced up at the others. "She's on her way."

She didn't think she imagined the sense of calm

that swept through them all. Emma had that way about her of making people feel as if everything was under control even if it was utter chaos.

"Come on," Lindsey said to Sully. "Let's get those cuts washed out."

He rolled up from the ground and put his arm around her shoulders, then he pulled her close and kissed the top of her head. "Not gonna lie—that was a bit intense for a moment."

Lindsey laughed. "Agreed."

When they were back inside the house, she marched him straight to the sink, where she began to wash the cuts and scrapes. Sully looked amused by her nursing him, but Lindsey thought he should count himself lucky that she didn't wrap herself around him as tight as a boa constrictor, she was so relieved he was all right.

"I don't mean to sound ungrateful," Chloe said. "Because believe me, your timing was spectacular, but how did you know I was being attacked, and how did you know to arrive here when you did?"

Lindsey glanced up from where she was blotting a particularly nasty cut on Sully's hand. They were all quiet, as if no one wanted to admit that it was sheer dumb luck. There was no point in prevaricating.

"Actually, it was just great timing. We were on our way here to talk to you about what you know about Grady's past," Lindsey said. "We thought maybe you could tell us who the third woman is."

"Third woman?" Chloe asked.

"In his shed," Lindsey explained. "There were pictures and mementos of you, me and a third woman. Her picture was under a shelf."

Chloe stared at her. "Oh, yeah, the shrines." She shivered, and Lindsey resisted the urge to do the same. "I don't know who the third woman was. I told Chief Plewicki I'd never seen her before, and I haven't."

"It's odd, though, isn't it?" Robbie asked. "I mean, her picture was in the shed, but not a full shrine. And it was hidden, even more than your pictures were, as if there was an extra layer of secrecy about her."

"Like he didn't want his wife to find the pictures, but most especially, he didn't want her to find that one," Sully said.

"Maybe she was his first obsession," Charlie said. "If his wife found out about her, it might have caused a problem in their marriage."

"But who is she?" Lindsey asked.

They were all silent, mulling over who this woman could be and why her picture was in the cabinet but hidden. Chloe put down her bag of ice and moved over to the coffeepot. She held up the carafe in silent question, and they all nodded.

All except Robbie, who asked, "You don't happen to have a nice oolong or Darjeeling, do you?"

"Sorry, no," Chloe said. She began to prep the coffee. Looking over her shoulder as she filled the carafe with water, she said, "The only commonality between you and me is our interest, or rather our perceived interest, in Grady's roses. I would think that the woman in the picture, whoever she is, must also be tied to the rose community somehow."

"Maybe Trudy Glass from the Berkshire Rose Club knows who she is," Lindsey said. "I can call her and send her the picture if she's willing to take a look at it."

"You have the picture?" Chloe asked.

"I might have snapped a quick picture of it when Emma was called away," Lindsey said.

"What? That's crossing a line, Lindsey. You're messing with my girlfriend's investigation," Robbie said.

Lindsey stared at him.

"Well, I have to have some outrage on her behalf, don't I?" he asked. "Don't tell her I said this, but nice work."

Lindsey shook her head.

"If it turns out the woman in the photo shot Grady, you both have to be careful," Sully said. "That picture is old, and who knows what she looks like now. She could be in Briar Creek, and we'd never even know it."

"You're right," Lindsey said. "Let's keep this between all of us."

"Who am I going to tell?" Chloe opened her arms wide to encompass the house.

Lindsey made a mental note to encourage Chloe to come into town for the night. She could stay at the house with her and Sully until they knew it was safe. Any thoughts she'd had about Chloe being Grady's killer were vanquished by the fact that Chloe had almost been killed.

"What do you remember about Grady's back-story?" Lindsey asked.

"Not much. I didn't really do any background research on him," Chloe said. "The piece was about the rose club, not Grady. He just thought it should be about him and his roses."

"So no deep biographical study?" Robbie asked.

"No, in fact, when he started to get weird, I tried to avoid using him in the article as much as I had planned to, because I didn't want him to get the wrong idea."

"Which probably didn't work," Charlie said. He shook his head. His man bun had been knocked loose, and his hair swept down across his shoulders. "Stalkers never get it."

Robbie stared at him in disbelief. "You've had stalkers, plural?"

"They're called groupies in my industry," Charlie said. He bobbed his head as if listening to some beat the rest of them couldn't hear and then smiled at Chloe, clearly trying to charm her. "I'm a musician."

She blinked at him.

"Okay, so we don't have much background information," Lindsey said. She cut in before the smoke from Charlie's crash and burn choked them all. "I think the very first thing we should do when we get out of here is to find out everything we can about Grady's personal life."

Chloe wrinkled her nose as if the idea had a bad smell attached to it, but she shrugged in reluctant acceptance. "All right. I can review my notes and see if I have any contacts to follow up with who might know something."

"Who might know something about what?" a voice asked from the open back door.

15

They all turned around to see Emma Plewicki and Officer Kirkland enter the house. They were both in uniform and looked windswept, hot and tired. Lindsey figured this case had to be running them into the ground.

"Anyone who might know something about Aaron Grady," Lindsey said. She wasn't going to lie. She had too much at stake—namely, Sully's freedom—to pretend she wasn't one hundred percent invested in figuring out who had killed Grady. "We're trying to figure out who from his past might know the identity of the lady in the picture that was under the shelf in his gardening shed."

Emma shook her head. "I might have known you wouldn't let this go."

"Sorry, not sorry," Lindsey said.

Emma, to her credit, laughed. "It's all right. I showed the picture to Sylvia, and she had no idea. She was completely unglued by the pictures of you two in the cabinet. She even went so far as to say that you two broke into the shed and put the pictures there yourselves. She seems to think you planned the murder together."

"Oh, that is too much," Robbie said. "I understand denial as much as the next guy when I don't get what I want, but that is just lunacy. For what possible reason would these two put their pictures in his shed?"

Everyone glanced from Emma to Robbie and back. Emma blew out a breath and said, "Mrs. Grady seems to think that upon her husband's rejection of their advances, Lindsey and Chloe got together, murdered him and then made it look as if he'd been harassing them to absolve themselves of the crime."

"That is . . . that's . . . I can't . . ." Chloe stammered, clearly struggling to form a sentence.

"Exactly," Lindsey said.

"I agree," Emma said. "But let's deal with the situation at hand. What happened here?"

They all looked at Chloe. She recited to Emma exactly what she had told them. Emma listened intently and then nodded at Kirkland. He pulled on a pair of gloves and headed upstairs to examine the room where Chloe had been attacked.

Emma then turned to Lindsey, who had retrieved the coffeepot and was filling mugs and passing them around with spoons and the sugar bowl while Chloe grabbed a jug of milk from the refrigerator.

"And what made you decide to come and visit Chloe?" she asked. She took a mug of coffee, black, and sipped the scorching-hot brew without even wincing.

"We came to find out what Chloe knew about Aaron Grady," Lindsey said. "We thought there might be something in his past that would shed a light on who wanted to kill him."

"I get that you have a vested interest," Emma said. She glanced at Sully, Chloe and then Lindsey. "I do, but you need to leave this to the police. His killer is still out there, and it looks as if they have decided to make one of you look like the guilty party."

Lindsey and Chloe exchanged a look. Emma was right. Whoever had killed Grady had felt desperate enough to try and stage a suicide. If Lindsey and her crew had been any later getting here, they might have succeeded.

"Speaking of which"—Emma turned to Chloe and continued—"I don't think you should stay here alone. We have access to a safe house. Would you be willing to stay there until we get this situation resolved?"

"Yes, please." Chloe wilted a bit against the counter. "I was planning to go stay at the bed-and-breakfast in town if need be."

"You're always welcome to stay with Sully and me, too," Lindsey said.

"Or you could crash with my aunt," Charlie offered. "She's great about taking people in, and I live right above her."

Chloe looked a bit teary at all the offers. "Thank you," she said. "Really, I so appreciate it, but I think the safe house might be the best place, since they've already tried to kill me once. I couldn't stand it if I put anyone else in harm's way."

"If you're sure," Lindsey said. "But if you change your mind, even if it's in the middle of the night, our offer stands."

"Thank you," Chloe said.

Emma interviewed each of them. When a crime scene technician arrived, ferried by Ian in the water taxi, Emma gave them leave to go. Chloe stayed so she could pack and take her laptop once it was dusted for fingerprints. Robbie opted to stay, too, wanting to be with Emma even though she warned him not to get in the way.

Charlie hopped into Ian's boat, leaving Sully and Lindsey to return alone in their boat. Lindsey watched over her shoulder as they pulled away and the house got smaller and smaller. She couldn't shake the feeling that whoever had tried to harm Chloe was now going to be feeling even more desperate to turn suspicions away from themselves, but who was it, and why had they chosen Chloe to be their fall guy? It could just as easily have been Lindsey. But there was more history with Chloe, and she had been on an island by herself. A perfect target.

"She'll be all right," Sully said. He seemed to understand her worry.

"I know," she said. "Emma will take care of her. I just feel unsettled by everything."

"Understandable," he said. "Come here."

Lindsey hopped out of her seat, figuring he was going to give her a hug. He didn't. Instead, he slipped out of his seat and nudged her into it. Then he put her hands on the wheel.

"Let's go for a ride and blow the cobwebs out."

He showed her how to operate the throttle, and Lindsey carefully increased the speed just a little. She turned away from the islands, and Sully helped her navigate around the remaining ones until they were clear and cruising out into Long Island Sound.

Lindsey cut the wheel so that they were headed east, toward what she always thought of as the "big water," as in deep, dark and scary. While she had no desire to ever swim in it, she loved being on the boat.

Sully reached over and nudged her. He raised his voice to be heard over the wind. "Let her rip!"

Lindsey didn't need to be told twice. She moved the throttle to a higher speed until they were skimming across the tops of the waves. The wind was whipping at her hair, and the cold splashes of water coming off the bow felt like heaven. She took them farther and farther out, and when she glanced at Sully, he just grinned at her.

She turned sharply to the left, or port side as the

sailors said, and they bounced across the water like a stone skipping across a pond. The sheer force of the wind and the water and the power of the engine in her hands made her laugh out loud. She'd always known that Sully loved the sea, and she'd even understood why. It was a glorious and terrifying mistress he had, and she knew that every day he took his boat out, it made him feel alive.

But Lindsey had never tried to master the ocean. She'd never felt the call to the sea, but at this moment, when fear and death had been plaguing her for weeks, she felt the cathartic release of the wind and waves. It felt as if the ocean air was blasting all her troubles off her. She circled back in the direction of the bay. She enjoyed one more long jagged burst of speed, and then she downshifted into a slower gear.

The sun was beginning to set. She scanned the water for the large red buoy that marked where they turned into the bay. When they drew close, she slowed down even more and turned the wheel over to Sully. She wasn't foolish enough to think she could navigate the islands when it was already getting dark.

As they switched places, she hugged him tight. "Thank you. That was amazing."

"You're welcome." He kissed her head and let her go. He slid into the captain's seat, and they puttered into the bay, cruising around the islands without kicking up a wake, until they were at the pier.

Lindsey jumped out onto the dock to tie up the boat, and Sully secured it for the night. Together they climbed the stairs up to the pier. Once they were up top, Lindsey paused to look at the bay and out beyond at the sound. She felt renewed and refreshed, as if she'd wiped the slate clean and was starting all over again.

It hit her then that maybe that was what Aaron Grady had been doing. Married to Sylvia for years, had he been trying to wipe the slate clean? Was that why he'd become obsessed with Chloe and then with her? Had he been trying to start over? If that was the case, what did he think he was going to do with the wife he already had?

"What are you thinking about?" Sully asked.

"Grady's text to Chloe," she said. "She said that he wrote that he thought June first would be a great day for a wedding, but he was already married. What do you think he planned to do with Sylvia?"

Sully squinted out at the darkening sky. "There aren't many options if he wanted to get married again. He'd have to divorce her or wait until she died, unless . . ."

"Unless he planned to help her with that," Lindsey said. "Do you think she suspected?"

They exchanged a look.

"Emma said Sylvia had a rock-solid alibi," Sully said. "Do we know what it was?"

"Something about being away at a work conference," Lindsey said. "I'm sure Emma checked out her story and someone must have corroborated it."

"Unless she had an accomplice," Sully said. "The person who slammed into me on that island was strong. Now, it could have been a woman in a panic, or it could have been a man who was helping her."

"That makes so much sense," Lindsey said. "What if Grady wasn't the only one who wanted out of the marriage? What if Sylvia wanted out, too? She could have had her lover kill him while she was away and then tried to frame it on me or Chloe. And if you think about it, maybe it was Sylvia who found out that Chloe had come here, and she moved here, too, planning to reunite Grady with his obsession, so that he would leave her or she could leave him, but it didn't work out that way. Maybe Grady found out about her and her lover, and she had to kill him."

"Whoa, whoa, whoa." Sully held up his hands. "The theories are flying fast and furious."

"I know, but I think we might be onto something," Lindsey said. "I don't think Sylvia is as innocent as she pretends."

"Perhaps not," Sully said. "But there's still the dilemma of finding out who the woman in the photo from the cabinet is. She could be our killer. She could be the one trying to frame you and Chloe, which would make sense if she killed Grady."

"But who is she, and why would she kill him?" Lindsey asked.

"I think that's where we need to start," he said. He took her hand, and they walked up the pier. "So, librarian, any idea where we can take that picture to have it circulated to possibly identify the woman?"

"We may not have to. I have an idea but it's a real long shot," she said. "I'm thinking I want to try and do a reverse image search."

"This is possible?" he asked. They arrived at his truck, and he unlocked the door and opened it for her.

"Yes, in fact, I just helped a young woman unload a poseur the other day by using it to prove that the person chatting with her online was using an Australian model's picture as his profile pic. Of course, in this case, it depends upon whether that woman has had her picture posted on the internet, but if she did, we might find a match." Lindsey climbed into her seat.

"That kind of freaks me out," he said. "In an oh-my-God-there-really-is-no-privacy sort of way."

"Says the guy who doesn't have a social media page," she teased.

"I have one for the business."

"That Charlie runs," she said. "Believe me, I'm not judging. I never go on social media either, and after all of this weirdness with Grady, I might delete all of my accounts. I'm beginning to feel like the most valuable things I possess are my privacy and my time."

"You're not wrong," Sully said. He closed her door and circled the front of the truck and climbed into the driver's seat. "How accurate is the reverse-image technology?"

"I don't know. I've only used it the one time, and it worked pretty well," she said.

"So it's possible." Sully let out a low whistle.

He started the truck and pulled out of the parking lot and onto the main road. Lindsey opened up her phone and searched for different reverse-image apps. There were several. Some charged a fee, but she figured she'd wait until she was desperate before she broke down and paid for a search. She opened her internet browser, the same one she had on her library computer, and loaded the picture of the mystery woman from Grady's shed.

She felt her heart hammer in her chest a bit as the search wheel spun. It took a minute, but several images were finally loaded. There was no match. There were images that were similar in composition but none that matched the picture Lindsey had uploaded. She did a search for different reverse image search apps and tried another one. This time there were no matches, but the website offered to go more in depth if she'd enter her credit card. Hard pass. She chose another website, and again, there were matches that they would be happy to share for her credit card info. Nope. She opened another just as Sully was pulling into the driveway.

She uploaded the photo and hopped out of the truck while the website did its magic. Sully led the way up the stairs to the house. As soon as he opened the door, Heathcliff made a beeline for Lindsey, practically knocking the phone out of her hand in his need to get to her.

Lindsey stopped staring at the screen and gave Heathcliff her attention. She kissed his head and told him he was a good boy. Then she rubbed his ears and his belly. When he was satisfied, he flopped down on the ground in front of Sully for more of the same.

While the menfolk went through their greeting ritual, Lindsey glanced down at her phone. She stared at the results and frowned. It showed one hit. She figured it would be another mistake. She opened up the page that the image linked to, and her heart dropped into her feet. There was no mistake.

The image matched the picture of the woman from Grady's gardening shed exactly and her name was listed as Mrs. Sylvia Grady.

16

Y ou all right?" Sully said. "You look pale."
Lindsey turned her phone around so he
could see the article.

"What?" He rose to his feet and took the
phone. He scanned the article. It was a wedding
announcement for Aaron and Sylvia Grady from
twenty-eight years ago. "How is this possible?
This is not the Sylvia Grady we know. There's no
way. Even with age, her hair and eye color are
wrong, and so is the shape of her face. This isn't
her."

"I agree," Lindsey said. "Off the top of my
head, I'd say it's a mistake. Maybe the wrong
picture was published with the announcement, or
maybe he married twice and both women were
named Sylvia."

Sully shook his head. "This is bad. Really bad.
If it was a mistake, why did he have the picture
in his shed?"

"Maybe he got attached to it when it ran in the
paper," Lindsey speculated.

Sully looked dubious. He led the way into the
house, stepping into the kitchen while Lindsey
leaned against the doorjamb.

"I planned to ask Trudy Glass, the woman from the Berkshire Rose Club, if she recognized the woman in the photo," Lindsey said. "Maybe she knows something about the picture or what it might have meant to Grady."

"Worth a shot," Sully agreed. He glanced around their kitchen as if trying to remember why he was there. Then he looked at her and asked, "Frozen pizza for dinner?"

Lindsey gave him a thumbs-up. "How about beverages for an appetizer? It's been a heck of a day."

"I'll start pouring," he said.

Lindsey wandered into the living room. She had called Trudy from her office before, so this time she had to look up the number of the rose club and hope that it was tied to Trudy's personal phone. She didn't want to wait until tomorrow.

She hit the link to call from the website and waited. Sully brought her a glass of wine. Their eyes met and she shrugged.

"Hello." A woman answered the call, and Lindsey recognized Trudy's voice.

"Hi, Trudy?" she said. "This is Lindsey Norris. We spoke the other day about your rose club."

"Oh, hello, Lindsey," Trudy said. "What can I do for you?"

"Well, I have another question for you," Lindsey said. "I have a photograph of a woman who we are trying to identify, and I was wondering if you could take a look at it?"

"Oh, all right," Trudy said. "Is there any reason you think I might know her?"

"She's known for enjoying roses, and I think she might be from your area," Lindsey said. It was vague, but maybe it would be enough.

"Oh, okay," Trudy said. "Can you send it to my phone in a text message?"

"Sure," Lindsey said. She tried not to get excited, knowing that Trudy might not recognize the photo. "To the same number?"

"Yes, please, I'm on my cell."

"All right, let me see." Lindsey opened her photos and quickly texted the picture to Trudy.

She heard the other woman's phone chime.

"Just a sec, let me grab my glasses," Trudy said.

There was a pause, and Lindsey could hear rustling noises. Then there was silence. For a moment Lindsey wondered whether they'd been cut off, but Trudy came back on the line.

"I don't understand," she said. "Why are you sending me a picture of Mrs. Grady?"

"Excuse me," Lindsey said. "Could you repeat that?"

"That's Sylvia, Aaron's wife, although the picture looks much older than when I knew her," Trudy said. "I think one time she told me that they'd been married for over twenty-five years."

"Really?" Lindsey asked. Sully had put the pizza in the oven and was back, sipping his beer and watching her with raised eyebrows.

"Yes, she and Aaron went to high school together in Maine, somewhere around Bar Harbor, if I remember right," she said. "Aaron often talked about how the thick fog that rolled in from the ocean made growing roses effortless up there."

"Maine—Sylvia and Aaron Grady were originally from Maine?" Lindsey asked just to clarify.

"Yes, that's what they said," Trudy said. "I'm sure of it."

"And you are absolutely sure that the woman in the photo is Mrs. Sylvia Grady," Lindsey said.

"Absolutely, she used to make the best lasagna at the club Christmas party every year, with little sausages. It was always a favorite," she said.

"Thank you, Trudy, you've been a huge help," Lindsey said.

"Oh, well, I'm happy to," Trudy said. "Mrs. Grady isn't in trouble, is she? I know Aaron was killed, but she didn't have anything to do with that, did she? I always liked her. She was so patient and kind. I'd hate to think that something has happened to her."

"Truthfully, I'm not sure," Lindsey said. "But I promise if I learn anything, I'll let you know."

"Thank you, I'd appreciate that," Trudy said. "You should come see our rose show at the end of the summer. It's really quite spectacular."

"I'll keep that in mind," Lindsey said. She was just being polite. She didn't think her relationship with roses was ever going to recover after all of this.

The call ended, and she tossed her phone onto the coffee table and took a long sip of wine.

"I take it Trudy recognized the picture as Grady's wife, Sylvia," Sully said. His voice sounded as grave as Lindsey felt. "And there's something about Maine?"

"The Gradys were from Maine before they moved to the Berkshires," she said. "So the reverse image search was correct, and the woman in the photograph is Sylvia Grady."

Lindsey put down her glass and picked up her phone again. She opened the wedding announcement, which was from June first, nineteen ninety. She studied the accompanying picture, which was just of Sylvia and matched the one in the shed.

She thought it was odd that Aaron Grady wasn't pictured. But there was no doubt that Sully was right. This Sylvia was not the Sylvia they knew. The shape of the face was different, and so were the eyes and hair. She scanned the brief information. The wedding was in Bar Harbor, which matched what Trudy had said, and it listed Sylvia as working for a company called Sunrise Health Insurance, while Aaron Grady was an economics professor at the local community college. Lastly, the article mentioned that the couple would be relocating to the Berkshires in Massachusetts where they'd start their married life together.

"This makes no sense," she said. "The woman we know as Sylvia Grady is definitely not this Sylvia Grady."

"You don't happen to have a photo of the current Sylvia to do a reverse image search with, do you?" Sully asked.

"No, darn it." Lindsey frowned.

The oven chimed, and Sully went to fetch the pizza while Heathcliff jumped onto the couch and propped his head on her leg. Lindsey absently rubbed his ears while she thought about all she had learned. She suspected Emma already knew the identity of the woman in the photograph, but Lindsey sent her a text anyway.

She kept it short and said that she'd done a reverse image search on the picture from the gardening shed and that the name that came up was Sylvia Grady and it was tagged to a newspaper article that announced her wedding to Aaron Grady. She also said that Trudy Glass of the Berkshire Rose Club confirmed the identity.

Sully reappeared with their pizza on two plates and sat down beside her, skillfully avoiding Heathcliff's nose as he tried to get a good sniff of their dinner.

"Your dinner is in your bowl," Sully said. Heathcliff perked up at that and scampered off the couch to the kitchen, where his food and water were kept.

"I texted what we learned to Emma," Lindsey said. She leaned back against the couch and took her plate from him. "How mad do you think she's going to be?"

"Hard to say," Sully said. "Mostly, she just gets mad if you put yourself in danger. She takes her oath to serve and protect very seriously."

"Which is why we love her," Lindsey said.

"Agreed," he said. "Maybe we'll get lucky, and Robbie will learn something useful while he's on the island with her."

"You're right," Lindsey said. "It's almost like having a liaison in the police department."

"Until we know more, you'll need to remain on your guard," he said. "I almost asked Emma if she could put you in a safe house, too."

"There is no house safer than this one," she said. Sully smiled, but it didn't quite cover the worry in his eyes.

She took her empty plate and his into the kitchen. Then she called to Heathcliff to go outside before they locked up the house for the night. She let Heathcliff out the back door and stood on the deck while he ran around the backyard. There was just the slightest breeze coming in from the ocean, and she hoped it was a sign that the drought might end and some rain would come their way.

The door opened behind her, and Sully joined her. She smiled at him and said, "Not letting me out of your sight, huh?"

"Not anytime soon," he said. He put his arm around her and pulled her close, and Lindsey wished it could chase away the feeling of unease that had dogged her since they'd found Grady's body. It couldn't. Nothing could until they discovered who had killed Grady and why.

Lindsey didn't hear from Emma that night, confirming her suspicion that Emma already knew what she had uncovered. In the morning, she dressed for work in the coolest clothes she could find: a white cotton blouse and skirt in a decidedly bohemian style. She brought a sweater with her because she knew the building and her office in particular would be cold once the air-conditioning got cranking.

Sully dropped her off at the library, waiting in his truck until she was safely inside. Ms. Cole had arrived before her, and Lindsey followed the scent of freshly brewed coffee into the staff break room, where she poured herself a cup. After greeting Ms. Cole, she holed up in her office to make some calls.

Her first call was to the rose club near Bar Harbor. No one answered, so she left a message.

Then she did a quick search for Sunrise Health Insurance's offices and noted they had offices in Bar Harbor and the Berkshires. It seemed likely that Sylvia had transferred her position instead of quitting. Lindsey wanted to talk to someone who had known Sylvia. If she'd worked for the company for years, maybe they could shed some light on what had become of her. When the website came up, she gasped. Their logo, a medical insignia in front of a sunrise, was familiar.

She tried to remember where she'd seen it. It had been on a suit jacket. A patron? One of her coworkers? No, she'd been outside when she saw it. Then she remembered it had been the current Sylvia who'd been wearing it, the day she'd accosted Lindsey and Chloe. Did that mean she worked for Sunrise Health Insurance, too? Could Grady have married two women who worked for the same company who were both named Sylvia? She was getting a weird feeling about all of this.

There was only one way to find out. Lindsey placed a call to the company. It was early, but maybe she could talk her way into some information.

"Good morning, Sunrise Health Insurance, how may I direct your call?"

"Hi, I'm checking the references for an employee who used to work in your offices," Lindsey said. "A Sylvia Grady? I'd like to speak with whoever her supervisor used to be, if I could? I'm sorry—I seem to have misplaced the direct number."

"That's all right. I remember Sylvia. Such a nice lady. I was so sad when she transferred to Connecticut. Her supervisor was Jean Handler, and she's here, so I can put you through. One moment, please," the woman said.

"Great, thanks." Lindsey felt as if she'd just cleared a hurdle. She hoped she could bluff her way through this conversation.

"Hello, this is Jean Handler. How can I help you?"

"Hi, my name is Lindsey Sullivan," Lindsey said. She blinked. She hadn't planned to use a fake name, but it seemed like a good idea. Still, she had never said what would become her married name out loud before. In fact, she'd never even thought about it, but now that she heard it, it sounded pretty cool. But wait, was she going to take Sully's name? She didn't know. This was one more wedding decision for which she was unprepared.

"How can I help you, Ms. Sullivan?"

Lindsey shook her head. *Focus!* "I'm calling to check on the references of one of your former employees, a Sylvia Grady."

"Sylvia, oh, she was such a lovely woman," Jean said. "How is she? Is she enjoying Connecticut? Has her health improved? We were all sad when she had to transfer so quickly from Western Massachusetts to the Connecticut shore."

"Well, she certainly seems robust," Lindsey said. "I'm calling because we're considering her for a position of employment, and we just wanted to hear what your thoughts were when working with her."

"Sylvia was an exemplary employee," Jean said. "She was fast, thorough and efficient. She took on other people's work when they fell behind. She was a real team player. Honestly, when she left, it felt like someone had severed my right arm."

"Why did she leave again?"

"Her allergies," Jean said. "They got so severe she was in the hospital. The doctor's orders were for her to move to a place with less pollen, so her husband packed her up and off they went."

"Just like that?" she asked.

"Pretty much. Aaron absolutely doted on her, always bringing her flowers from his garden, or he'd surprise her with lunch," Jean said. "But then she got sick. One day she was here, and the next she was gone, taking a lateral transfer to the Connecticut office. Even her team had no idea she was going to be leaving us."

"Do they still work there?"

"Let me think," Jean said. "This was a little over a year ago. I know that one of them left at the same time she did, giving no notice, which was a huge hit to the department, but the other two are still here."

Lindsey tried not to sound too eager when she asked, "Do you have their names? Just in case we need to do more in-depth research."

There was silence on the other end of the call, and Lindsey wondered whether she'd overplayed her hand.

"Who did you say you were with again?" Jean asked.

"The town of Briar Creek, actually," Lindsey said.

"Oh, a government job, I get it," Jean said. "You can't be too careful."

"Exactly." Lindsey forced a laugh that she hoped didn't sound too strained.

"Let's see. The woman who left at the same time was Ava Klausner, so she won't be able to help you, but the other two, Sonya Davids and Chrissy Sellers, they're still here."

"Great," Lindsey said. She wrote down the names, putting a star beside Ava Klausner since she found it odd that she'd left at the same time as Sylvia.

"Was there anything else I can help you with?" Jean asked.

"That's it, thanks," Lindsey said. "I'll be in touch if I have more questions."

"I'll be here," Jean said. Her tone was full

of resignation, as if this was her lot in life and would be for years to come.

Lindsey ended the call and immediately opened up the internet browser on her computer. A quick search for Ava Klausner turned up nothing, which was weird. Usually professional people showed up on corporate networks, if nothing else. She checked the other two names and found listings for both of them.

She debated whether she should go deeper into her search or whether she should just hand over the names to Emma. She knew that would be the mature and responsible thing to do, but the need to know was like a worm in her head.

There was a knock on the door, and she glanced up to see Ms. Cole standing there.

"Hi," she said. She noted Ms. Cole was frowning. "Is everything all right?"

"I'm not sure." Ms. Cole's color choice today was shades of yellow, making it a very chipper if somewhat eye-watering ensemble. "This message was left for you on the library voice mail."

Ms. Cole handed her a pink phone slip, and Lindsey noted that it was from Emma, asking her to drop by the police station as soon as she got in.

"Huh." Lindsey glanced at the clock. She had a half hour until the library opened. "I guess I could go over there now."

"It doesn't feel right, though, does it?" Ms. Cole asked. She paused in the doorway and lowered her glasses. She glanced at Lindsey over the top edges. "Emma is your friend. Why would she leave a message on the library voice mail and not your office number or, even more likely, your cell phone?"

Lindsey lowered the note in her hand. She reached into the purse she'd dumped in her bottom drawer and checked her phone. There was no message from Emma.

"You're right—that is odd," Lindsey said. "I think I'll call and verify this message. Thank you."

Ms. Cole gave her a quick nod and then went back to checking in materials. Lindsey picked up her cell phone. She was feeling edgy all of a sudden and even scanned the library, looking for anything amiss, but all was normal. It was just her and Ms. Cole in the building, which was still locked. They were safe.

She called Emma's cell phone. Emma picked up on the third ring.

"Lindsey, I don't have time right now," Emma said. "I know you're upset, but this has to be done according to protocol."

"I'm sorry?" Lindsey said. "What are you talking about? I'm returning your call."

"I didn't call you," Emma said. "I'm sorry, but you can't do anything here. I have to take Sully in, and you are just going to have to trust in the system."

"What?" Lindsey cried. "What do you mean, 'take Sully in'?"

"Oh, I thought you were—" Emma cut herself off. "I'll have him call you when we're at the station."

"No, you tell me what's going on now, Emma," Lindsey said. "As my friend, tell me what's happening!"

"I'm sorry, Lindsey." Emma's voice was low. "Ballistics matched the gun found at the scene as the same weapon that killed Aaron Grady, and it's been identified by serial number as belonging to Captain Michael Sullivan. I have to arrest him, Lindsey. He doesn't have an alibi. I have no choice."

Lindsey slumped back in her seat. She felt as if all the air had just been sucked out of her body.

"Emma, wait. Let me talk to him," Lindsey demanded. Silence greeted her. Emma had already hung up.

Lindsey jumped out of her chair. Her coffee was forgotten on the desk as she grabbed her purse and hurried out to the main room.

"Ms. Cole, something has come up," she said. "Have Ann Marie cover the reference desk when we open, and I'll be back as soon as I can."

Something in her face must have warned Ms. Cole away from asking questions, because she merely said, "Okay."

But she was speaking to Lindsey's back as

Lindsey dashed down the narrow hall toward the staff exit. She banged through the heavy metal door and out onto the sidewalk. The air was even more oppressive than it had been earlier, and she took a soggy gulp of it as she prepared to jog to the police station and get to the bottom of things.

Lindsey had her phone in hand and was trying to call Sully. It went right to voice mail. Why hadn't he called her to tell her what was happening? She tried Beth's number, but there was no answer, probably because she was headed to work and wouldn't get any notifications while en route. Then she tried Robbie. He answered on the first ring.

"I know you're upset—" he said.

"Upset?" she cried. "You know as well as I do that he didn't do this. How could Emma—"

"You know she has to do this by the book precisely so it doesn't look like there's any favoritism," Robbie said.

"Yes, but—" Lindsey began but was cut off when a car screeched to a stop in front of her. Thinking it might be Charlie or Ian coming to get her, she glanced up, leaving herself completely unprepared when the driver popped out of the car and slapped her phone out of her hands with the butt of a gun. "What the—!"

The driver was wearing a black hooded sweatshirt with the string of the hood pulled tight around their face and aviators. Just as Chloe had described her attacker. Panic made Lindsey's heart about stop.

"Robbie! Help!" she cried as she began to back away. She hoped the phone could pick up her voice. "Chloe's attacker is here—"

Lindsey turned to run. She was seconds too late as the gun came down hard on her temple. The ground flew up at her face, and everything went black.

17

It was the overpowering smell of roses that roused her—well, that and the throbbing in her temple, which felt like a hammer trying to pound a hole in her skull from the inside. Lindsey put her fingers on the pain place, half expecting to find something lodged in her head. There was a bump, and when she lifted her fingers away from it, they were sticky with blood.

She could feel it then. The blood. It was caked on the side of her head. It matted her hair and ran down her jawline in a crusty smear. Her eyes blinked against the daylight. She was lying on a path, a narrow walkway between towering trellises of roses. Looking up made her dizzy, so she glanced back down at her clothes. Her white skirt and blouse were dirty and covered in blood. She'd managed to lose a shoe.

She scanned the area. As far as she could tell, she was alone. But that wasn't right. Why go to the trouble of knocking her out and dragging her wherever she was just to leave her alone? Still, her flight response was kicking in as her heart rate increased.

She pushed up to her hands and knees. The

grass beneath her hands was dry and brittle and stuck to her sweat-soaked skin. Her breathing was ragged and she was shaking. She felt dizzy and woozy, but she didn't want to let the opportunity to escape pass her by. She tried to figure out which way to go. She couldn't see anything beyond the towering trellises of roses. Their big fist-sized blooms mocked her with their cheery profusion of petals in every color, from the purest white to the darkest crimson. The smell was overpowering, and she felt as if she was choking on the pungent sweetness.

She stood on wobbly knees and moved in the direction where her feet had been. She figured if she'd been dragged in here, then her feet would be pointing in the direction from which she'd come. It wasn't much of a theory, but it was all she had.

Her balance came back with every step she took, and she started to move more quickly, striding through the mazelike bushes until the roses were a blur in her peripheral vision. She rounded one corner and then another. Her heart was beating fast now, thumping with each step she took closer to freedom. When she turned the third corner and found herself staring up at a wall of thorny roses, her elation was smashed flat. It was a dead end. She turned around and went in the other direction, certain that this time she'd get out. Four more turns and she was at another dead end.

A disembodied laugh sounded over her own rasping wheeze. It was a mocking laugh, the sort a cat would make when it had a mouse cornered in a cupboard. It made the hair stand up on Lindsey's arms.

"You didn't really think you were going to be able to get out of here, did you?" the voice, a woman's, asked.

Lindsey didn't know where to look. She couldn't tell where the voice was coming from, but it was clear that there were cameras out here and someone had been watching her try to find her way out. The thought of it made her furious, which was a hell of a lot better than being afraid. She hugged the feeling to her middle, letting it spark her courage, like a torch pushing out the darkness and letting in the light.

"What do you want with me?" she asked.

The laughter started up again. Lindsey whipped around in a circle, making certain no one was sneaking up on her. It was then that she saw the blinking eye of a camera and the tiny speaker attached to it.

"You're so smart, librarian—why don't you tell me what I want from you?"

The woman's tone was mocking, as if she knew she had all the power. Well, to hell with that. Lindsey glanced around, looking for something, anything to use as a tool. There wasn't much. Thick rose bushes covered the wooden trellises that formed row upon row of the crazy maze she was in. She had once been in a cornfield maze when a storm blew up, and she and her friends had been stuck while hail rained mercilessly down on them. She had decided not to be a victim and had pushed through wall upon wall of corn until she busted right out the side of the maze.

The roses were too thick and the wooden trellises that supported them were too strong for her to just bust through them, but that didn't mean she couldn't go up and over. She looked for the thinnest patch of roses, and then she went in. Ignoring the thorns that clawed at her clothes and skin, she used the trellis to hoist herself up. It was slow going, as she had to search for spots to grab, plus she was missing a shoe, adding to the challenge.

"Hey!" the voice shouted. "What are you doing? Stop that!"

Lindsey ignored her. If she was getting upset, then Lindsey was on the right path. She hauled herself up, gritting her teeth when a thorn dug into her palm. The trellis was sturdy, and once she reached the top, she saw that the four-by-four top of the trellis was clear. Someone had kept the roses meticulously pruned to stay below the top edge. With a laugh, Lindsey looked around her. She was standing on a trellis in the middle of a rose maze in the back of what she now recognized as Aaron Grady's yard. Oh no.

"Hey! Get down!"

Lindsey ignored the voice and eyeballed the shortest distance between her and the edge of the maze. She began to pick her way across the top of the trellis, trying to hurry and keep her balance, neither of which was easy, as she was missing a shoe, had a throbbing headache and was hampered by the roses, which scratched her skin, tugged at her skirt and slowed her progress.

Lindsey didn't bother looking for the woman. She knew who it was. It had to be Sylvia Grady 2.0. She must have been the one who'd jumped out of the car and clocked Lindsey on the head. Given the outfit choice—the black hoodie and sunglasses—she now knew for certain who Chloe's attacker had been as well. Lindsey could only guess why Sylvia wanted her. With Chloe in a safe house, there wasn't anyone else to frame for Grady's murder.

Sylvia must not have known that Sully had been taken into custody this morning. That was a problem for Lindsey, as Sylvia likely figured she still needed a suspect. No matter. As soon as Lindsey could find a phone, she was calling Emma to come and collect the lunatic who had attacked both her and Chloe and had undoubtedly shot and killed Aaron Grady. In the meantime, Lindsey was on her own.

She reached the end of the row and saw the long

winding drive to the main road ahead of her. The roses were thick here, and climbing down was impossible. She decided to jump and hope she didn't break anything while sticking the landing. She didn't hesitate. She just jumped. The ground was hard, and she fell to her knees as a shooting pain caused her ankle to buckle. She gritted her teeth and forced herself back to her feet. She had to hurry. She took quick steps toward the road ahead.

With every step, Lindsey thought she might actually make it. She wondered later whether it was the blood loss that had made her such a cockeyed optimist. As she stepped out of the cover of the rose maze, Sylvia Grady appeared in front of her, holding the same gun she had clobbered Lindsey with. By Lindsey's count, this was the third gun Sylvia had pulled on someone. The woman must really love her guns.

"Don't move," Sylvia said.

She was still wearing the black hooded sweatshirt, but the hood was down and she wasn't wearing the sunglasses. Still, given her height and build, there was no doubt that she was the one who had attacked Lindsey outside the library. But why? When Sylvia failed to make it look as if Chloe had committed suicide, she must have realized that anything she did was going to be suspect.

"Whatever you think you're going to do, it's

not going to work," Lindsey said. "The police arrested Aaron's killer this morning."

"Right," Sylvia said. "As if I'd believe you."

Lindsey shrugged and then winced. Now that she was standing still and not running for her life, even the smallest movement made her head hurt.

"Suit yourself, but if you kill me and stage some elaborate confession, you'll just be giving the police somewhere to look other than at Sully, who is in jail even as we speak," she said. "That's where I was going when you grabbed me."

Sylvia's eyes narrowed. She didn't believe Lindsey, but would she risk harming her and having it ruin what might already be in play? Lindsey doubted it.

"Come on," Sylvia snapped. She gestured with the gun for Lindsey to walk.

Lindsey thought about breaking into a run. If this had been a corn maze instead of a rose one, she might have given it a try, but there was no quick escape here. She started walking. She noticed that Sylvia was keeping her distance.

"Why did you kill him?" Lindsey asked.

"Shut up," Sylvia said. "You're going to be dead soon. I have no reason to explain anything to you."

"No, but it would be the civil thing to do," Lindsey said. "I mean, if you're going to kill me. You should at least explain why, Sylvia—or should I call you Ava?"

Sylvia's chin tipped up. She looked taken aback, as if she hadn't thought anyone would be able to figure out that she was an imposter. Lindsey decided to push her advantage.

"You are Ava, aren't you?" she asked. The words tripped over themselves as she panted for breath, winded from her frantic climb up the trellis and hurting from the jump. "What happened, Ava? Did you kill Sylvia, or did Aaron? Were you two having an affair? I know you worked with Sylvia at Sunrise Health. How did you manage to take her identity within the company? How did they not figure it out?"

"Shut up, shut up, shut up!" Ava waved her gun at Lindsey. "You don't know anything!"

"I know the real Sylvia is dead, and I know you're not her," Lindsey bluffed. She glanced over her shoulder. "I know everything."

For a second—a nanosecond, really—a look of panic swept over Ava's face. Then she scowled. Frustrated, she grunted and shoved Lindsey so hard in the back that she stumbled to the ground. Her head was throbbing, and she was pretty sure her clothes were done for, but she was still alive.

"How'd you figure it out?" Ava asked. She paced around Lindsey where she was sprawled on the ground, half pushed up on her arms and ready to flee if given half a chance. "Did Rosie rat me out?"

Lindsey had no idea who Rosie was, but she

figured this was the opening she needed to stall for time and try to figure out what was going on in Ava's obviously unstable brain. She just had to remain calm. She could find a way out. She was sure of it.

"Yeah, Rosie told me everything," she said.

"Ha!" Ava scoffed. She leaned toward Lindsey. "Nice try. Rosie doesn't exist. You're a moron, trying to trip me up with lies and guesses. Well, it won't work."

Lindsey gritted her teeth. Her misstep seemed to make Ava more confident, and she grabbed Lindsey by the arm and hauled her to her feet.

"I just need to hide you," Ava said. "Until I know if they're going to arrest your boyfriend or not. If they do, well, you'll just have to disappear from the shame of it all."

"No one will believe that," Lindsey said. "I would never abandon Sully."

"Is that so?" Ava laughed. "Then maybe that cute British actor friend of yours will have to disappear, too. Maybe the two of you ran off together. Oh, yes, that could totally work. Oh, even better, I'll kill Chloe and make it look like the two of you ran off together. It's her fault I'm here, after all."

"Her fault?" Lindsey asked. "What did Chloe have to do with you coming to Briar Creek? Did Aaron follow her? Is that why you tried to kill her and make it look like suicide?" Ava shook her head, and Lindsey said, "No, don't deny it. I know it was you. You're wearing the same outfit you wore when you attacked her."

"You," Ava spat. "None of this would have happened if you hadn't turned Aaron's head. I had a plan. When he moved us to be near her, I decided to kill Chloe, preferably right in front of Aaron so that he would know never to look at another woman again, but then you flirted with him and got him interested in you, too."

"I did not flirt with him," Lindsey argued. She knew it was pointless. Ava wasn't going to acknowledge what she said, but she couldn't let such a horrible statement stand without challenge.

"Right." Ava's sarcasm was thick enough to spread on toast. It made Lindsey furious.

Before she could argue further, Ava shoved her hard in the back, forcing her to walk again. They were going in the direction of the shed, and Lindsey knew if she didn't break free before they got there, she wasn't going to survive to talk about it.

She glanced at Ava over her shoulder. "You won't get away with this. Chloe is safely hidden from you, and if you hurt Robbie, well, believe me, if he goes missing, Emma won't rest until she finds him."

"She won't find him," Ava said. She rolled her eyes, but it looked overdone. She was edgy. The bodies were stacking up, and it was going to be harder and harder to hide her crimes. This gave Lindsey a surge of hope. She just had to play it right.

"I left messages with what I've found, Ava. You won't be able to get away with killing Sylvia and Aaron," she said. "Adding me to the list is only going to make it worse for you."

"I didn't kill Sylvia," she snapped. "Aaron did."

"I don't believe you," Lindsey said. She was lying. She'd seen Aaron at his obsessive worst. She had no doubt he was capable of killing, but she wanted Ava to keep talking, and she knew being contrary was the way to make that happen.

"He did kill her," Ava insisted. "That's how I became her."

Lindsey slowed her pace and Ava did, too. Lindsey was hoping to take as long as possible to get to the shed, where who knew what sort of nightmare was awaiting her.

"I don't understand," Lindsey said.

"I don't understand," Ava mimicked her in a singsong voice. "What's not to understand? He got sick of her and wanted to ditch her for the little reporter hottie, but Sylvia refused to be dumped, so he strangled her. When she didn't show up for work after a couple of days—he'd been calling out sick for her—I went to their house. That's where I found her dead in her

271

bed. She was posed as if she was sleeping, but she wasn't. She was dead with marks around her neck like she'd been strangled. It was clear he needed someone to become Sylvia."

"Oh God," Lindsey said. The horror of what Ava was telling her was chilling. Aaron had murdered his wife to pursue Chloe, and when Ava caught him, she decided to become Sylvia. It was madness. "Why? Why would you pretend to be his wife? You were supposed to be her friend."

"Because I wanted her life. It was better than mine. So I made a deal with him. I would help him hide the body. I wouldn't tell anyone that he'd killed her. And I would become his wife, pretending to be her and covering up his crime. He would go free, and I would get a husband."

"So you were in love with him?" Lindsey asked.

"No," Ava scoffed. "It was her life I wanted. The house. The husband. He could have been anyone, but when I knew he'd murdered her, I knew I had him—for life. But he couldn't quite forget Chloe, now could he? When I discovered he'd moved us here to be near her, I knew I'd have to kill her, but then you showed up, and he became obsessed with you. I knew then that it was always going to be somebody he wanted— somebody that wasn't me."

"So you killed him." This was worse than anything Lindsey might have imagined.

Ava's gaze narrowed. "You talked to Jean, didn't you?"

Lindsey didn't want to say, afraid that Ava would add the woman to her hit list, so she said nothing.

"It doesn't matter," Ava said. "As soon as someone else goes down for the murder, I'll leave the area. I have enough money to go wherever I want. I really liked having a husband, though. I suppose I'll have to find another one."

"You can't be serious," Lindsey said. "You aren't going to be able to walk away from this."

"Sure I can. As far as anyone knows, I'm Sylvia the sad widow. Nothing is going to change that."

"I already have," Lindsey said. "I'm a librarian. We have access to all sorts of information, including reverse image searches, which is how I discovered the picture of the real Sylvia, information which I shared with the chief of police. She's going to call Sunrise Health in the Berkshires and figure out that you're a fraud, just like I did."

"Damn it, I said shut up!" This time when Ava went to shove her, Lindsey was ready. She dropped to the ground, propelling Sylvia right over her. Lindsey thought about wrestling her for the gun, but her head was pounding and her flight response had kicked in. All she could think was to take off running and get to a phone. She stomped on Sylvia's gun hand, hoping she broke it, as she broke into a sprint.

Her head was throbbing. The air was hot but a breeze had kicked up. Lindsey glanced up and noticed the sky, which had been a pale scorching blanket of white heat for weeks, was now thick with ominous dark gray clouds that blocked the sun. There was a distant rumble of thunder, because of course there was.

Lindsey dashed around the house and ran for the car. She could hear Sylvia shouting behind her. She yanked the driver's door open, hoping Sylvia had left the keys in the ignition. She had! Lindsey pressed down on the brake, switched the car on and put it in drive. She stomped on the gas and shot down the driveway, spraying gravel in her wake. A gunshot sounded and the back window exploded. Lindsey let out a noise between a yelp and a shriek and ducked down so that she could barely see over the dashboard.

Once she reached the road, she didn't even slow down but shot out onto the street, making a sharp right as she floored the gas and headed into town. She was almost there when a police car popped up in her rearview mirror. She didn't slow down. She didn't stop. She drove right into the police station with the squad car on her tail. She pulled into a spot, rolled down her window and put her hands on the wheel. She finally took a breath.

"Don't move or I'll shoot," a voice ordered.

"I'm unarmed," Lindsey cried. She glanced out the open window to see the dear familiar face of Officer Kirkland. His thick thatch of red hair was hidden by his hat, and his freckled face took on an expression of confusion.

"Lindsey! How did you—oh wow, are you okay?" He reached for the door handle and opened the door. He held out his hand and Lindsey took it.

"We've been looking all over for you," he cried. "Ms. Cole at the library called to say that someone in this type of car had abducted you. Your head! You're covered in blood! Are you going to pass out? Here, let me carry you inside."

"No, I can walk—" she began, but he cut her off, swooping her up and into his arms as he strode toward the building. He took the steps at a fast jog and hit the button for the door to open automatically.

"Really, I look worse than I feel," she said. She was pretty sure that was a lie. She felt lousy.

He ignored her. As soon as he cleared the door and stepped into the lobby, he shouted, "We've got a code twelve."

Karen Hobart, the desk clerk, looked up and her eyes went wide. "On it!" she cried and picked up her phone.

"Code twelve?" Lindsey asked. "What's that? Are you going to put me down?"

"Officer Kirkland, what's going on—" Emma

came striding up from the back. At the sight of Lindsey, she staggered. "Oh, thank God. Bring her in back. Call an ambulance, then call Sully and Robbie and tell them we've located her. Let them know she's here and she's okay."

The desk clerk gave her a thumbs-up. Kirkland hustled Lindsey into the break room, putting her gently down on a chair, while Emma popped the lid on a metal first aid kit and sifted through the contents.

"What's going on?" Lindsey asked. "Sully's not here?"

"I'll explain," Emma said. "First things first, you're covered in blood."

"Yeah, about that," Lindsey said. "Sylvia, although that's not really her name, is your killer, not Sully."

"I know," Emma said. "That's why he's out looking for you with Robbie."

"You have to warn them away from the Grady house!" Lindsey cried. "She had a gun. She'll shoot them. She tried to shoot me."

"Karen is calling them in—don't worry," Emma said.

"How did you get away?" Kirkland asked.

"She went to shove me, I ducked, she fell, I stomped on her arm and ran for the car," Lindsey said. "Listen, she's not Grady's wife. She's an imposter. Her name is Ava Klausner, and she worked with Grady's wife at the insurance agency. She discovered he murdered his wife and used it to blackmail him into pretending she was his wife."

"Should I head out there, Chief?" Kirkland asked. Emma nodded. He ran from the room.

Emma's eyebrows shot up. "How did you figure all of this out? Besides the reverse image search that you did. Sully told us about that."

"This morning, I reread the wedding announcement, and it mentioned that Sylvia worked for Sunrise Health," she said. "When I looked up their website, I saw they have an emblem that looks like a doctor's seal with a sun behind it. I remembered the day we ran into Ava after Grady's body was discovered. She was wearing a lapel pin with the same symbol.

"So it occurred to me that the connection between the Sylvia we know and the former one was the job. I figured whoever this woman was, she had to have worked with Sylvia in the office up in the Berkshires, so I called them and pretended I was doing a reference check. I got Sylvia's former manager, and she listed three people but said one of them had left after giving no notice at about the same time that Sylvia had put in for a medical leave and then a transfer to the Connecticut office. That person was Ava Klausner. When I told Ava what I knew, she said it didn't matter, because I wasn't going to live long enough to tell anyone."

"She was wrong," Emma said. Then she grinned and held up a fist. With a weak smile, Lindsey gave her a knuckle bump. A commotion sounded from the front of the station, and then Sully was there, charging into the back room as if he were planning a jailbreak.

18

He didn't stop or slow down. Instead, he scooped Lindsey up and hugged her tight. "Are you all right? Do you have a concussion? Are you bleeding? I'm taking you to the hospital."

"Stop." Lindsey laughed even though it made her head pound. "Now that you're here, I'm fine." She hugged him tight. "I've never been better."

He cupped her face and studied her pupils as if to make sure they were the same size. Then he took in the gash on her head and the dried blood.

"Here." Emma slapped some antiseptic wipes into his hand. "You're the spouse-to-be—you can do cleanup. I need to put an APB out to all the surrounding towns to be on the lookout for Ava Klausner, a.k.a. Sylvia Grady." She looked at Lindsey. "Any idea where she might have gone?"

"No, but call the local Sunrise Health Insurance office," Lindsey said. "Ask if there is anyone there who worked with Sylvia Grady, specifically someone named Rosie."

"Rosie?" Emma looked intrigued. "As in Rosie Donovan, the coworker who told us Sylvia was with her at their insurance adjusters' conference in Providence at the time of Aaron Grady's death?"

"Yes," Lindsey said. "Ava thinks Rosie rolled over on her. When she asked if Rosie had blabbed, I bluffed and said I knew all about her. And then she recanted, pretending there was no Rosie. But if there really is a Rosie, she might be in danger now."

"Got it," Emma said.

A sudden boom of thunder erupted, and they all jumped. Lightning flashed, and a deluge of rain came down on the police station. The lights went out, flickered once, and then went out again.

"Damn it," Emma cursed. "I don't have time for this."

"Come on," Robbie said. "Let's go find some flashlights."

"They're in the emergency kit out at the front desk," Emma said. Robbie left the room, banging into a chair on the way and letting out a curse as he went.

"You two stay here," Emma said over her shoulder to Lindsey and Sully. "I still want to get the word out about our suspect, but I want to know you're safe."

"I took Ava's car, and I didn't see another one at the house," Lindsey said. "She has to be around there somewhere."

Another rumble of thunder sounded, and they

all started. The fierce wind rattled the windows, and the lightning lit up the room for a second.

"I'll be back," Emma said. She strode toward the door, tripping on the same chair Robbie had and muttering the same curse.

Sully waited until she cleared the room, and then he pulled Lindsey close and held her as if he just needed to reassure himself that she was okay. Lindsey leaned into his embrace. The thought that Ava might have gotten her way and ended her life just when she was getting to the good stuff was a bit more than she wanted to deal with right now.

She leaned back and looked at Sully. She could barely make out his features in the gloomy half-light, but she met his gaze and said, "Let's elope."

"I knew it!" a voice cried from the doorway.

Lindsey whirled around, which caused her to be completely unprepared for the ball of wet black fur that came charging at her. Heathcliff jumped for her, and she would have been knocked on her keister, but Sully was there, bracing her with his strength.

A flashlight shone in their direction, and they shielded their eyes. "You owe me five dollars, Vi."

"Fine." The flashlight was turned up toward the ceiling, and it illuminated the room.

"Hey, buddy." Lindsey rubbed Heathcliff's ears

and glanced up at the door to see her crafternoon friends Nancy and Violet standing there. "What are you two doing here, and with Heathcliff?"

"Well, I was getting ready to do some baking when the storm blew in," Nancy said. She glanced at her friend with a look of gratitude, and Lindsey knew without them telling the rest of the story what had happened. Storms were the boogeyman for Nancy. Having lost the love of her life when his boat went down in a surprise storm, she struggled whenever an unexpected one hit.

"But I arrived at her house and told her that it was not the time for baking—we needed to go get Heathcliff," Violet said. "You know how dogs hate storms, and we didn't want him to suffer."

Lindsey glanced down at her furry little man. He was wagging away, completely oblivious to the thunder and lightning. She glanced up at the two ladies.

"You heard I got kidnapped, didn't you?" she asked.

"I might have overheard something on the local police scanner while I was trying to dial in the weather forecast," Violet said.

"Right," Sully said. "And how did you know to come be here?"

"I heard there was a code twelve, a call for an ambulance, for someone at the police station. Given that I knew Lindsey had been nabbed,

I was hoping it was for Lindsey. Not in a life-threatening way but rather in a superficial-injury, we-saved-you-from-a-bad-guy sort of way," Violet said.

"And if it was you, we figured you'd need Heathcliff," Nancy said.

The two women moved forward and nudged Sully out of the way. They took over cleaning Lindsey's cuts and scrapes, and Nancy even produced some over-the-counter pain-reliever tablets from her purse and pressed them on Lindsey.

As she relaxed into a chair, the muscles she had used to climb the trellis in her escape attempt began to ache, and she was grateful to her friends for their care.

The storm raged on. Sully put on the radio, and they listened to the local news reports about the weather. There was no information about Sylvia, a.k.a. Ava. As the time ticked by, Lindsey became more and more concerned about what the woman would do. It occurred to her that if Sylvia was out for revenge, she might try to find Lindsey at the library, and any person in her way could get hurt.

She borrowed Sully's phone and called Beth. There was no answer, so she assumed Beth was busy dealing with the power outage. She called the main desk, hoping to get Ms. Cole. Again, there was no answer. She felt her heart start pounding in her chest. She counted the rings. Eight, nine, ten. She ended the call.

Pushing out of her seat, she glanced at Sully. "Something's wrong at the library. They're not answering the phone."

"The power's out," Violet said. "Maybe the phones aren't working."

"The desk phones are on a landline," she said. "They should work."

"I'll go. You stay here," Sully said. She looked at him and he sighed. "Fine, but you stay with me at all times."

"What? Where are you two going?" Nancy asked. Her eyes were wide, as if she couldn't imagine going out into the storm.

"The library," Lindsey said. "We have to. Will you and Violet keep Heathcliff here with you?"

"Yes, of course, but don't you think you should tell Emma?"

"We will," Lindsey said. "But my people are at the library, and if Ava goes after them, looking for me, I can't live with that."

She felt an urgency to be gone, to be at the library, so strong it made her bounce on her feet. She glanced down. She was still missing a shoe.

"Here," Violet said. She toed off her own flats and pushed them toward Lindsey with her foot. "We're about the same size."

"Thank you," Lindsey said. She smiled at her friends as she and Sully hurried from the room.

Karen was alone in the front when they arrived. She told them that Emma and Kirkland were out searching for their suspect and that Robbie had insisted on going with Emma.

"We're going to the library," Lindsey said. "If Emma calls, tell her that."

"You're not supposed to leave," Karen said. She looked flummoxed, as if this was a complication she hadn't expected. "I can't let you leave."

"I'm sorry, but you have no choice," Lindsey said. "My people aren't answering at the library, and I'm worried that they're in danger. Call Emma and tell her—I don't care, but I can't stay here."

Karen picked up the phone and nodded. "Go. I'll call. The safety of our residents has to be our number-one priority."

"Thanks," Lindsey said.

She and Sully dashed out into the rain. Sully had snagged a spare umbrella from the bucket by the front door. It was an extra-large one and kept them mostly dry from the waist up, but the wind whipped the rain sideways, soaking their legs and shoes.

"What's the plan?" Sully shouted over the wind and rain.

"Back door," Lindsey said. "I can type in the code to get us in. If Ava is there, I don't want her to know we're coming."

"Got it," Sully said. He took her hand, stepped off the sidewalk and cut across the side yard of the police station, through the dead grass, to a service road that led behind the buildings on Main Street. They followed it until they reached the narrow patch of trees that opened up into the parking lot of the library.

They had to turn the umbrella sideways and walk in single file to get through the trees. When they arrived at the parking lot, Lindsey noticed that it was empty save for a few cars she recognized as belonging to her staff.

Per library protocol, when there was a power outage, the library would close. She knew that her staff would have waited until whoever was in charge—it had been Ms. Cole in Lindsey's absence—declared that the library needed to close for safety concerns. Then they would make certain every patron was out of the building, and they would lock up until the power came back on or they were excused for the day.

She clenched her fingers into fists, fervently hoping that that's what had happened. She supposed the phone line could have gone out, but she doubted it.

They dashed across the parking lot and into the recessed area of the staff entrance. Sully closed the umbrella while Lindsey lifted the cover of the keypad and tapped in the security code. She heard the lock disengage, and she went to open the door. Sully muscled her out of the way, however, and opened the door slowly, quietly slipping into the library.

Lindsey followed, noting that Sully was now holding the umbrella like a weapon. The lights were out, with only grainy diffused light coming from the windows as the storm raged on. Her wet skirt clung to her legs and felt cold as the air seeped into the fabric, chilling her skin. She felt her teeth chatter, and she didn't know whether it was because of fear or cold, but she clamped her jaw together so as not to make any noise.

They reached the end of the short hallway, and Sully paused. He reached back and pushed Lindsey against the wall. She waited while he cautiously peered around the corner. She strained to hear anything. The punchy sound of the small receipt printers, a squeaky wheel from a book truck, the clunky metal *ka-chunk* of a footstool being stepped on, Beth's infectious laughter, the sound of Ms. Cole shushing someone, the swish of the doors opening and closing. There was nothing. Not a sound. It felt as if the life had been sucked right out of the library. It was terrifying.

If it hadn't been for the cars in the parking lot, she would have believed her staff had left the building, and she would have been relieved. But she recognized the cars as belonging to her staff. The power outage had lasted long enough that they should have left the building by now, but they obviously hadn't, and why weren't they answering the phone?

"Where should we check first?" Sully asked.

"The break room," Lindsey said. "If they're here, I would imagine they're waiting in there."

He nodded. They crept through the main library, sticking to the shadows. It felt as if every corner hosted a possibility of danger, and Lindsey kept glancing over her shoulder, half expecting something or someone to jump out at her.

But nothing happened, and she felt her tension ease just a bit. They moved through the work-room and toward the break room. The library remained silent except for the slosh and squish of their rain-soaked shoes. There were no sounds of voices talking, which Lindsey found alarming, because her staff members were not known for their quiet demeanors. Even the lemon had a pretty loud shusher when she was irritated.

As they approached the break room, Lindsey grabbed Sully's arm and held him back. She leaned close and whispered, "Something's wrong. It's too quiet."

He nodded, and she knew he had been thinking the same thing. It was then that she heard the click. A lock? A door shutting? She wasn't sure. Sully pulled her into the shadows, and they waited for another sound so that they could deter-mine where it was coming from, but there was nothing.

And then Lindsey felt the press of something hard against the back of her skull. She gasped, and Sully whipped his head around. His eyes went wide and Lindsey knew. It was Ava, and she was right behind Lindsey.

"Don't move, sailor," Ava said. "Or I'll shoot your pretty wife-to-be. After all, I've got nothing to lose. Move your hands where I can see them."

Sully lifted his hands out away from his body.

"Drop the umbrella," she said.

She pushed the barrel of the gun into the back of Lindsey's head, making her cringe. Sully dropped the umbrella. Lindsey felt Ava's hand reach up and grab her by the back of the neck. The barrel of the gun moved so it was right beside Lindsey's head and trained on Sully.

"You're the reason my husband is dead," Ava hissed in Lindsey's ear. "It would be only fair for me to shoot him in revenge. Eye for an eye, husband for a husband and all that."

The fear rocketing through Lindsey in that moment almost made her ill. She couldn't let Ava hurt Sully. She'd rather take the bullet herself. She met Sully's gaze and mouthed the words *I love you.*

19

Sully's eyes went wide, but as if he could read her mind, he dived to his left just as Lindsey used her elbow to drill right into Ava's midsection. The woman doubled over, and as she went down, the gun went off, its boom ricocheting through the empty library as it made Lindsey's ears ring.

Lindsey grabbed Ava's hand and dug her fingers into the fleshy part just like Emma had taught them, forcing her to drop the gun.

"Stop!" Ava yelled at Lindsey.

Sully jumped up and grabbed Ava's arms, hauling them behind her back. She was still wheezing, but she fought and thrashed, kicking out at him until he managed to hold her wrists together while also standing clear.

"Where is my staff?" Lindsey stood in front of Ava and stared at her. It took everything she had not to grab the woman by the throat and shake the answer out of her.

Ava looked up at her with her gray hair mussed and her glasses askew, and she snarled, "They're dead. I killed them all."

Lindsey staggered back a step. She shook her

head in denial. Her voice was mostly air when she whispered, "No."

Ava laughed, a spine-chilling cackle that made Lindsey's entire body go cold. Beth, Ann Marie, Ms. Cole, Paula. No, she couldn't—she wouldn't—believe it.

She turned away from Ava and ran. She exploded into the break room, expecting to see carnage. There was none. She whirled out of the room and began to check the library—the study rooms, the story time room, every row, every nook, every cranny. There was no sign of anyone, dead or alive.

"Lindsey!" Sully called after her. "Wait. You don't want to find them alone—"

She ignored him. She loved him with all that she was, but this was her staff. She was responsible. Tears and sobs began to pour out of her as she careened toward the crafternoon room, the last unchecked area. If anything had happened to them, well, she didn't think she would survive it.

She pushed open the door to the crafternoon room. A flash of lightning illuminated the room just enough for her to see several shadows sitting in the circle on the floor. In the harsh light her eyes met those of her dearest friend. But it was dark again, and she couldn't tell, she didn't know, whether Beth was dead or alive.

She dropped to the floor and crawled forward. Using her hands to find her, she felt a pair of shoes. When her fingers landed on Beth's shin, Beth bucked and Lindsey realized she was alive! She traced the side of Beth's body up to her face. She felt her jaw and then the curling edge of a piece of tape. With shaking fingers, she ripped the tape off.

"Oh, thank you," Beth cried. She gulped in air and then said, "It was Sylvia Grady. She's crazy. She wants to kill you. Lindsey, you have to run. Go. We'll be all right."

"No, it's all right. Sylvia—rather, Ava—has been caught. She'll never harm anyone again," Lindsey said, her voice catching, her relief was so great. She felt for the others and one by one pulled the tape off their mouths.

There were a few sobs, but mostly, everyone was gasping for breath. Lindsey moved around them, trying to break the tape that bound their feet and hands. Her fingers were weak, and she couldn't see.

"I'm going to get some scissors," she said. "Don't move."

"Really?" Ms. Cole asked. Her tone was dry.

Beth was the first one to laugh, and then Paula and Ann Marie joined her. It took Lindsey a second in her fuzzy, panicked head to get the joke, and then she did a facepalm and groaned.

"I'm sorry," she said. Then she laughed. It was full of relief and gratitude, and she said, "I'll be right back."

She dashed out of the room and hurried back to the main room. Sully was standing there with Ava, and Lindsey almost burst into tears when she said, "I found them. They're tied up but they're okay."

In the dim light, she saw Sully's shoulders slump in relief. "Excellent."

He was still holding on to Ava and was unable to move, as she would be still for a moment and then try to drop to the ground or wriggle free. He had to stay on his guard to keep her secure.

"Here, I think we have some zip ties that we use for keeping the computer cords together," Lindsey said. She opened a cupboard and grabbed a few of the ties and joined Sully.

"You can't do this," Ava said. "I'll have you arrested."

They ignored her, and once Lindsey pulled a tie tight around her wrists, Sully crouched to do the same around her ankles. She tried to kick him in the head, but he was stronger and captured her feet with one hand while Lindsey secured the tie. Ava couldn't move. Sully grabbed a nearby chair and none too gently pushed her into it.

"I'm going to free the others," Lindsey said. "Will you call Emma?"

"On it." Sully was already pulling his phone out of his pocket.

Lindsey opened the main drawer of the circulation desk, where Ms. Cole kept all her supplies, including scissors and a stapler with her name written on pieces of masking tape adhered to their sides. Normally, Lindsey was afraid to touch Ms. Cole's supplies, but she was operating on the rule of closeness here and figured Ms. Cole wouldn't mind just this once. She grabbed the scissors and raced back to the crafternoon room.

While she cut the tape from their wrists, they poured out the story.

"We had just sent the patrons and the part-time staff home," Beth said. "We were calling the mayor's office to see if they had any news on the power outage, when that woman grabbed Ann Marie and told us she would shoot her if we didn't do exactly as she said."

Lindsey glanced at Ann Marie. She looked shaky but otherwise all right. She squeezed her hand, and Ann Marie gave hers a quick squeeze in return.

"She forced us in here and then used this duct tape to tie us up," Ms. Cole said with a sniff. "We would have fought her, but she was very clever. She had us tape each other's hands while she held the gun on Ann Marie. Then she had us sit in a circle and forced her to tape our ankles."

"Yeah, it was like a bad team-building exercise," Paula said. She was the first one freed, and she popped up to her feet and began to stretch.

"Then she taped our mouths," Ann Marie said. She stood, too. "She was waiting for you. She wanted revenge. She blames you for forcing her to kill her husband."

"He wasn't her husband," Lindsey said. She cut through the tape around Ms. Cole's ankles and helped her up.

"What do you mean?" Beth asked. Lindsey crouched to release her friend while the others began to walk around.

"Sylvia Grady isn't who she appears to be," Lindsey said. "Her real name is Ava Klausner, and she worked with Sylvia at an insurance company. Supposedly, she took the identity of Aaron Grady's wife after he murdered the real Sylvia, but I'm not sure I believe that. When Ava discovered Sylvia was dead, she decided to take her place."

"That's mental," Beth said. Lindsey grabbed her hand and pulled her into a standing position.

"Agreed," Lindsey said. "Sully's got her restrained, and Emma's on her way. Are you okay? She didn't harm you, did she?"

"No, I'm fine," Beth said. Then her voice wobbled, and she sobbed, "I'm just glad you are. Oh, Lindsey, I can't lose my best friend."

She wrapped Lindsey in a fierce crushing hug, and Lindsey hugged her back. If anything had happened to Beth and the baby, she'd never be able to live with it. Never.

"It's okay. We're all okay," she said.

As if awaiting their cue, the lights came on.

Lindsey glanced at the faces of her friends and coworkers, and then, as if it was the most natural thing in the world, she pulled them into a group hug. It turned into a huddle, where they had their arms around one another's backs and they were facing one another.

"You all performed above and beyond the call of duty," Lindsey said. "I will be sure to write up all of this in my report to the mayor."

"Him," Ms. Cole sniffed. "I don't give a flying fig what he thinks. None of this would have happened if he had stopped that little pervert from harassing you to begin with. He's been our mayor for too long. I think it's time someone challenged him this November."

She was staring at Lindsey with a fiery light in her eyes, and Lindsey felt her own eyes widen. There was no way, none, that Lindsey would ever consider a position in politics.

Paula gave Ms. Cole a sidelong glance and said, "You know, you're right. I'm new to Briar Creek, but even I know we've never had a woman mayor. It's about time."

"Yes," Beth cried. She bounced on her feet and clapped. "Someone with an impeccable code of honor and ethics, a person who loves this town and knows and values its history."

Lindsey's head swiveled in her direction, and then she glanced at Ann Marie. But Ann Marie wasn't looking at her; she was looking at Ms.

Cole, and she said, "How about it, Ms. Cole? I think 'Mayor Cole' has a lovely ring to it, don't you?"

Ms. Cole tipped her chin up and nodded. "Yes, yes, it does." She glanced at Lindsey with a wary glance. "What do you think?"

A million emotions rocketed through Lindsey. Joy that Ms. Cole was asking her opinion, as her doing so was amazing and showed just how far they'd come. Pride at the bravery it would require for Ms. Cole to throw her hat into the ring. And optimism at the thought that a woman might step up and take charge of their town, and the next time a person was harassed, maybe the town would be more concerned about the victim and less about a potential lawsuit from the perpetrator.

She looked at Ms. Cole and said, "I think you would make a fantastic mayor. You most definitely have my vote."

Ms. Cole met her gaze, and a small smile tipped the corner of her mouth.

"What?" Lindsey asked.

"You realize if I become mayor, then I'll be your boss," Ms. Cole said.

Lindsey smiled in return. "I can't think of a better one."

Ms. Cole's eyebrows lifted, and she looked embarrassed by the vote of confidence. "Well then, we should probably get out of here. The chief of police will no doubt want our statements about what happened."

With that, Ms. Cole swept from the room with all the self-important dignity of a mayoral candidate.

"Ms. Cole versus Mayor Hensen," Beth said. "And just when I thought things were going to become less interesting in Briar Creek."

"Things are never not interesting in Briar Creek," Paula said.

"That's a fact," Ann Marie agreed.

Lindsey watched as the two women followed Ms. Cole out to the main library. She fell into step with Beth and looped her arm through her friend's.

"Mayor Cole," she said. "It does sound good."

"Yeah, but she'll always be Mayor Lemon to me," Beth said.

She made a puckered face and Lindsey laughed. It was the first stress-free laugh she'd had in days, and it felt amazing.

20

W edding cakes?" Nancy asked. "Our crafternoon food is wedding cakes?"

"Don't laugh at me," Lindsey said. "I have all
of these samples, and I don't know which one to
pick. I'm having a cake meltdown."

"That is wrong on so many levels," Violet said.
She picked up a fork and tucked into an angel
food and strawberry confection that looked so
light, Lindsey expected it to float. "Why not let
Sully choose?"

"Cake isn't really his thing," Lindsey said.
"He said whatever I pick is okay with him. So
I've narrowed it down to these five cakes and
their fillings. We have an angel food cake with
strawberry, white chocolate cake with raspberry,
almond cake with chocolate, red velvet cake with
cream cheese and chocolate cake with mocha
cream."

"Mocha cream?" Mary came into the room
with Josie on her hip and made a beeline for the
table with the different cakes on it. Her eyes went
wide at the cakes, and she glanced up and asked,
"Is this heaven?"

Beth laughed as she tucked her fork into the

almond cake. "No, but it may be the new lunch menu for the crafternooners."

"This is glorious," Charlene said as she joined them. "If we're voting on it, I vote yes." She kissed her mother's cheek as she slid onto the seat beside her.

Lindsey said, "We need to table that vote until we decide which of these should be my wedding cake."

"While I am always happy to partake of cake," Paula said, "I think it's a very personal decision for your wedding. Maybe instead of voting, we can just help you suss out which is your favorite."

"That would work, too," Lindsey said. "But I'm at critical. The wedding is a few months away, and I have to start making some decisions or this is going to be the worst wedding in the history of weddings."

"No, it's not," Beth said. "All of the extras don't matter so long as at the end of the day, you and Sully are married and starting a new life together. Cake, dresses, dinner, flowers—all of that is just the cherry on top."

Lindsey blinked at her. "I don't want cherries on my wedding cake."

Beth dropped her head to her chest in feigned exasperation, and they both laughed.

"Seriously, if you ladies don't help me, there might not be any cake or flowers or music or . . ."

"All right, don't panic," Violet said. "I'm sure we can at least nail down the cake today."

"Thank you," Lindsey said. "Ms. Cole came up with a system. There are five cakes, so everyone tries a piece, a bite, or a nibble and then ranks them from one to five, with one being your first choice and five being your last. The cake with the lowest number will be my wedding cake."

"That's an excellent system," Nancy said. She glanced at Ms. Cole, who was standing off to the side. She stabbed a piece of the chocolate cake with her fork. "Very clever."

"Thank you," Ms. Cole said. "I'm working on my problem-solving skills to help with my run for mayor."

The cake fell out of Nancy's open mouth and landed on the table with a splat.

"Mayor?" Violet slowly turned away from the cakes and stared at Ms. Cole.

"I'm making a run," Ms. Cole said. She forced a smile that was more teeth than anything. "I hope I can count on your vote."

Violet drew herself up and looked Ms. Cole over from head to toe. She considered her from every angle and then gave a decisive nod. "Yes, you can, and I think I can help you present yourself in the best possible light."

"Mayor?" Nancy said again, looking as if she was still wrapping her head around the idea.

Beth put her arm around Nancy's shoulders. "I know. It takes a while. You'll get there."

"If anyone cares," Mary said, "I actually read this week's book, *Gaudy Night*, and I loved it. I don't care what the critics say—I really like Harriet Vane, and I don't think she detracts from the prior Lord Peter Wimsey books at all."

"She is a terrific character, especially when you consider the mystery was written in nineteen thirty-five and Harriet is described as struggling between her love of academia and her love for Wimsey. Did you know *Gaudy Night* is considered the first feminist mystery novel?" Lindsey asked.

"And the book nerd has arrived," Beth said. "All is right in our world again." Paula snickered, and they helped themselves to some cake.

"I love Sayers's entire series, especially when she describes the motorbikes," Charlene said. "Did you know she was a motorbike rider herself?"

"I did not," Violet said. "That seems like something I should know."

"The golden age of mystery writing, in between the wars in Britain, is captured so well by her," Paula said. "The plots are so very intricate."

Ms. Cole passed out the cake-rating cards, and Lindsey made sure everyone had a plate, a fork and a pen. She'd brought Greek salad skewers and a charcuterie board to balance out the sweetness of the taste testing, as well as a big jug of unsweetened iced tea.

"Speaking of intricate plots," Charlene said. "What is happening with Ava Klausner, a.k.a. Sylvia Grady? Last night was the first time the Grady murder wasn't on the news in days."

"She was arrested for murdering her husband," Lindsey said. "The car that I stole when I ran from her house was taken by the crime lab, and they found trace amounts of blood in the trunk that matched Aaron Grady. It's believed that she shot Grady in the shed behind their home and then loaded up his body and drove him into town, where she left him and the gun behind the library to make it appear that either I or Sully had shot him."

"But what about the footage of Grady stealing the gun from Sully's office?" Mary asked. "Do we know why Grady did that?"

Lindsey frowned. She took a bite of the angel food with strawberry filling, which also had a lovely whipped cream frosting, and marked it down as number two on her note card.

"According to Sylvia, Grady was planning to kill Sully with his own gun and make it look like a suicide, thinking that in her grief, Lindsey would turn to him for comfort, and then he would get rid of Sylvia—rather, Ava—and they'd live happily ever after," Beth said.

"But what about Chloe, the woman from the

newspaper that he was stalking?" Paula asked. "I mean, it can't have been a coincidence that Grady ended up in the same area as the woman he'd been obsessed with, right?"

"It wasn't," Lindsey said. "But in a weird twist, worthy of Sayers, it was Ava who decided to move near Chloe. Grady had no idea."

"Why would she do that?" Violet asked. "You'd think she'd want to be as far away from the other woman as possible."

"From what Ava told me when she was chasing me through their rose garden, her plan had been to move close to Chloe and kill her so that Grady would know she was dead and he'd get over his obsession."

"That is stone cold," Paula said. "And completely insane."

"Which is an excellent description of Ava," Lindsey said.

"What about his actual wife?" Nancy asked. "I mean, I heard that Ava said Grady killed her and she decided to take on her identity and assume her life, but how do they know if he did it or not? It could have been Ava who killed the real Sylvia."

"They've sent a forensics team to the former Grady residence in Tollenton, Massachusetts," Lindsey said. "According to Ava, they buried Sylvia's body in the woods surrounding the house. They're hoping to recover the body and be able to determine how she died. It may or may not prove Ava's story, but either way she will stand trial for killing her husband."

Lindsey supposed she should have felt badly about Grady's murder, but she didn't. She figured it was a lot like that line from Anne Lamott's book *Bird by Bird*: "If people wanted you to write warmly about them, they should have behaved better." She could not remember Grady as anything other than the scary, horrible person he was, and she wasn't going to beat herself up about it.

"Let's talk about something happy," Paula said. "All this murder stuff is making me glum. What else is left for you to decide for your wedding?"

"Not much, actually," she said. "Sully is in charge of music, our moms are taking on the decorations, Mary and Ian are in charge of the food, I have my dress, and Sully and I have planned our honeymoon. Oh, and Steve Briggs has agreed to officiate the ceremony."

"So that leaves just the flowers," Charlene said. "It's a Christmas wedding, so what are you thinking?"

In truth, Lindsey had no idea. She hadn't really thought about it yet. "I only know one thing for sure," she said. "I'll carry anything but roses."

The group looked at her in complete under-standing.

"How about forget-me-nots?"

Lindsey turned to face the door, and there was Sully. He was standing there, with his broad shoulders almost filling the narrow space, holding a vase that was overflowing with flowers—white hydrangeas with blue forget-me-nots. It was perfect.

As one, the entire crafternoon group let out a big feminine sigh of appreciation. Lindsey grinned at him and left the table to join him by the door.

She glanced down at the flowers. Simple, elegant, lovely, they were as untamed and wild as her sailor boy but also as serene as her librarian self. If ever two flowers represented two people perfectly, these were them.

"They're beautiful," she sighed. "What made you bring them?"

"I wanted you to have a better memory of a guy bringing you a vase of flowers than the one you currently have," he said. "I saw these in Kelsey Kincaid's shop, and I thought they'd do the trick."

"Best groom ever." Lindsey grinned up at him.

Sully smiled and his eyes crinkled in the corners. "This is nothing—wait until you see my husband game."

"It gets better than this?" she asked.

"Way better."

"Remind me—why aren't we eloping?" she asked.

"Because we are going to savor this," he said. "We've got a Christmas wedding and fabulous river-cruise honeymoon in our very near future. Nothing's going to stop us now."

Then he kissed her, and Lindsey knew he was right. They were finally getting married. What could possibly go wrong?

The Briar Creek Library
Guide to Crafternoons

What is a crafternoon? It's pretty much exactly what it sounds like. A gathering in the afternoon where participants get together to discuss a book they've read while enjoying a meal and doing a craft. Here are some suggestions to get you started.

Readers Guide for
Gaudy Night

by Dorothy L. Sayers

1. What is the role of academia in the novel?

2. Is Harriet's dilemma, her struggle between becoming a wife or remaining an academic, authentic? If so, why?

3. *Gaudy Night* is considered the first feminist mystery novel. Do you believe it is or not? Why or why not?

4. Sayers's protagonist, Lord Peter Wimsey, is of the nobility. How does this work for him as an amateur sleuth? Does it work against him at all?

5. What do you think Sayers was trying to say by choosing that particular person as the killer? Does the killer's reasoning seem plausible to you?

Craft:
Tin Can Lantern

Tin can (empty coffee can or soup can with labels
  removed)
Hammer
Awl
Towel

Fill the empty can with water and freeze overnight. Spread a towel to work on. Using a
hammer, tap the handle of the awl until it punc-
tures the can. Make as many holes as you want,
in a pattern or randomly. Once the ice melts,
wash the can and let it dry. Once it's dry, it can
be painted on the outside. When ready to use, put
sand in the bottom of the can and light a small
votive candle to place in the sand.

Recipes

CHARCUTERIE BOARD

An easy option for all sorts of gatherings, especially book clubs.

Using a large cutting board, arrange a wide variety of meats and cheeses and other delicacies on the board.

Meats (all sliced):
  Prosciutto
  Soppressata
  Salami
  Pepperoni
  Dry sausage

Cheeses (include a cheese knife):
  Gorgonzola
  Brie
  Mozzarella
  Gouda
  Havarti

Olives:
  Green olives stuffed with garlic or jalapeño
  Kalamata olives
  Black olives

Dried fruit:
  Apricots
  Dates

Nuts:
  Pistachios
  Cashews
  Almonds

Spreads:
  Horseradish
  Mustard
  Fig jelly
  Mini sweet gherkin pickles

Lastly, add a variety of breadsticks and crackers.

GREEK SALAD SKEWERS

1 big block of feta (about 12 oz.), cut into
  12 cubes
1 bottle Greek salad dressing
12 pitted Kalamata olives
12 cherry tomatoes
1 cucumber, cut into 12 large cubes
12 6-inch wooden skewers
Flaky sea salt
Freshly ground black pepper
Fresh dill

Marinate the feta cubes in the Greek dressing.
Take a skewer and slide on a cube of cheese, a
Kalamata olive, a cherry tomato and a cucumber
cube. Make 12 skewers. Sprinkle with salt,
pepper and dill to taste. Offer extra salad dressing
on the side.

WHITE CHOCOLATE CAKE
WITH RASPBERRY FILLING

(Lindsey's future wedding cake but also a
fun cake to make for any occasion)

3 cups all-purpose flour
1 tablespoon baking powder
½ teaspoon salt
4 oz. white chocolate, chopped
1 cup butter, softened
1¼ cups sugar
4 large eggs, room temperature
1 teaspoon vanilla extract
1¼ cups milk

Preheat oven to 350°F. Grease and flour two
round 9-inch cake pans. In a medium bowl,
whisk together flour, baking powder and salt.
Set aside. In a small, microwave-safe bowl, melt
the chopped white chocolate by heating it in
30-second intervals in the microwave. Stir well
with a fork between each interval. The chocolate
is ready when it's smooth when stirred.

In a large bowl, cream together butter and sugar.
Beat in eggs one at a time, followed by melted
white chocolate and vanilla extract. Alternately

add the milk and the flour mixture. Divide batter evenly into prepared cake pans.

Bake for 30 to 35 minutes or until a toothpick comes out clean or the tops spring back when lightly pressed with a fingertip. Let cool for 10 minutes, and then transfer the cakes to cooling racks to cool completely.

RASPBERRY SYRUP

7 cups raspberries, fresh or frozen (thaw slightly)
¾ cup lemon juice
1¾ cups sugar
2¼ cups water
1 teaspoon vanilla extract

Combine raspberries, lemon juice, sugar and water in a saucepan, and bring to a simmer over medium heat. Cook until raspberries are soft, about 15 minutes.

Strain raspberry mixture through a fine-mesh sieve, using the back of a spoon to press down to get all the juice through the sieve. Discard raspberry seeds, and pour extracted juices into pan. Simmer over medium-low heat until reduced by half or to the consistency of syrup, 20 to 25 minutes; add vanilla extract at the end of cooking time.

WHITE CHOCOLATE CREAM CHEESE FROSTING

8 oz. cream cheese, room temperature
½ cup butter, room temperature
2 oz. white chocolate, melted and slightly cooled
1 teaspoon vanilla extract
3 tablespoons milk or cream
4–6 cups confectioners' sugar
White chocolate shavings
1 cup fresh raspberries for garnish

In a large mixing bowl, cream together cream cheese, butter and melted white chocolate. Beat in vanilla and milk, then add in the confectioners' sugar gradually until the frosting reaches your desired consistency. Put 1 cup of frosting in a small bowl, and blend 1 tablespoon of the cooled raspberry syrup for the filling. Add more sugar if needed to reach desired consistency. Spread on top of the bottom layer of the cake. Carefully set the second layer of cake on top. Using a spatula, spread frosting all around the sides of the cake and along the top. The frosting should be a bit stiff to allow piping along the outer edge of the cake. Once the cake is completely frosted, transfer the remaining frosting to a pastry bag fitted with a star tip, and pipe a circle on the outer edge. Fill the circle with 1 cup fresh raspberries and white chocolate shavings. Drizzle the entire cake with the remaining raspberry syrup.

Center Point Large Print
600 Brooks Road / PO Box 1
Thorndike, ME 04986-0001 USA

(207) 568-3717

US & Canada:
1 800 929-9108
www.centerpointlargeprint.com